THE ADVENTURES OF CELESTE THE CAT

Celeste and the Giant Hamster

Melanie Typaldos

Dedication

To my granddaughter, Celeste, for inspiring me to write a book about cats. To my daughter, Coral, and son, Philip, for suggesting we get a capybara. And to Caplin Rous, my pet capybara, for being the incredible creature he is.

Chapter One
How (not) to catch a capybara

Celeste's dark form slid from the bed to the carpet. She could hear her human, also named Celeste, turn restlessly to fill the newly vacant pillow. Celeste knew her human dreamed of a cat who would stay with her through the night. Celeste thought this was ridiculous. Human Celeste had celebrated her ninth birthday some months before and cat Celeste thought it about time the young human overcome her childish fear of the dark. Anyway, if human Celeste wanted a pet to sleep with her, she should have gotten a dog. Cats were not made for such things.

Celeste hesitated in front of the hamster's transparent plastic home. The little ball of fur spun endlessly in its exercise wheel.

As she did every night, Celeste examined the door with the hope that her human had failed to secure it. She pushed the top section with her paw but it remained firmly in place. The rodent did not even pause to look at her.

The dwarf hamster was a constant source of humiliation for Celeste. No matter how hard she tried, she could not break into the hamster cage. Most of the other cats were nice about it; after all some of them had to share their homes with parakeets, guinea pigs or fish—all prey animals clearly not suitable for pets. But the other cats didn't know Celeste's secret, the shame she hid from every feline soul. What would the other cats think, what would they do, if they found out that human Celeste had named the creature Celestina? Celeste shuddered and left the room.

She trotted down the hall to the entry and opened the rubber covering of her special cat door to peer outside. She detected no movement in the hallway between the apartments or on the stairs leading up to the second floor where she lived. From above came the annoying clamor of rap music, muted by the floor and two walls, but still loud enough to cause her ears to twitch.

When she got to the bottom of the steps, Celeste found the regular group of neighborhood cats sitting on the fence between the apartment complex and the empty field that lay to the east. Mostly they consisted of rowdy tomcats, though some had good voices. When the mood struck her, Celeste would sit and listen, occasionally joining in. But tonight the human music and the feline accompaniment hurt her ears.

The moon hung nearly full in a cloudless sky and Celeste had better things to do than howl at it like a dog. No, this was a night for a prowl.

"Hey Celeste! Wait for me."

Celeste paused as a big orange tabby bounded up beside her. "Hi Tiger."

The striped cat purred loudly. "What a night, eh? You going out for a hunt?"

Celeste raised her tail straight in the air and resumed her steady pace through the parking lot. Tiger fell in beside her, his big paws making heavy thwaps as they hit the pavement. "A night like this is not to be wasted, Tiger. Feel the breeze, warm and wet like it's just blowing off the jungle."

Tiger's head bobbed. "Yeah, the jungle." Then after a while, "Celeste, how do you know what the air off the jungle feels like? You only ever lived here. Parking lots and roads. How come you know what a jungle is like?"

Celeste sighed. Like most of the local cats, Tiger didn't have much imagination. "Don't you ever listen to bedtime stories, Tiger? My human loves to hear stories about elephants and lions and little brightly colored frogs that spend their lives in trees."

"There aren't any kid humans at my house. Just two adults. And they never read out loud."

"Well, don't they watch TV? There's a whole channel on jungles and the animals that live in them."

"Nah. I mean, yeah, they watch TV but all it ever has on it is humans talking to humans. Whenever I try to watch with them, I end up falling asleep."

"That's probably the news. It tells humans what's going on with other humans." Celeste paused, one foot raised delicately above a small puddle. The recent rain had made the parking lot a treacherous obstacle course for a cat who didn't like getting her feet wet. "My adult humans watch it every day, morning and night."

Celeste twitched her ears with excitement. Like Tiger, she normally found the human news programs incapable of holding her attention. But the news this morning had been different. Its ridiculous claim of "news you can use" had finally proven true.

Celeste wasn't sure she wanted to share her information with Tiger. He was a nice enough cat and all, but he could hardly outsmart a mouse. She didn't want anyone to mess up her chances. Still, it would be good to have someone watch her back. And, intelligence aside, Tiger was a hefty cat with big claws to match.

"I heard," Celeste began, the tip of her tail switching, "there is a giant hamster loose in the field. Tonight we hunt big game!"

"A giant hamster? I don't know. Could any hamster be called big game? How big is this giant hamster, anyway?"

"Maybe really big. Maybe as big as a kitten." Celeste purred as she spoke. "If I catch that giant hamster I can show the whole fence-sitting gang what kind of cat I am." And, she thought, if I plop a big dead hamster down in front of human Celeste, she might at last understand that rodents are food, not pets. Her whiskers raised in anticipation.

"Where should we look?"

Celeste had been considering that question ev
learned about the giant hamster. That morning,
parents were watching the news while their daughter ate
breakfast.

"What's a capybara?" human Celeste asked.

"It's a giant rodent," her mother replied.

"A rodent?"

"Like your hamster, only bigger."

"A lot bigger. A thousand times bigger. I wonder how one got
loose," Celeste's father gestured at the TV.

"They said it was someone's pet," Mother replied. "Imagine
keeping something like that as a pet."

Celeste wound her way around the legs of the breakfast table,
asserting her presence to the adults. They finally voiced the
question she had thought so many times.

"Takes all kinds," Father said. "Better than keeping a
monkey, I suppose. But you'd have to have some sort of pond or
pool for a capybara. According to the newscast, they spend most
of their time in the water."

And that was why Celeste decided to start her search for
the giant hamster at the drainage pond where the field met
the apartment complex fence. There was plenty of water there,
especially since the recent rain. She told Tiger of her plan as
the two of them crept under a Jeep. She liked high-clearance
vehicles. She didn't have to crouch down to go under them. Of
course, Tiger was taller and still could not walk upright, but she
imagined it was easier for him too.

The water in the drainage pond shimmered in the moonlight as they approached the fence. Dense reeds and cattails grew in the far corner where runoff from the road drained into the pond through a large concrete pipe. Celeste thought the hamster would most likely hide in the tall plants.

"Okay, Tiger," she said as they slid between the narrow bars of the fence, "you go left and I'll go right. We'll meet on the opposite side. Give a call if you see anything."

Tiger flicked his ears in agreement and padded briskly off.

The air was humid from the rain and full of sounds from the pond. Frogs and toads croaked and chirped. A screech owl's sad call warbled in the distance. Celeste could even hear the tiny paw-pats of field mice walking on the floating leaves of the water lilies. She strained to hear the sounds of a giant hamster.

If a giant hamster sounded anything like a dwarf hamster, Celeste was all too familiar with their noises. All night, every night, she heard Celestina. For such a tiny animal, the hamster was surprisingly noisy. It made a variety of squeaks and chirps that humans apparently didn't notice but which were painfully annoying to cats' sensitive ears.

But mostly Celeste knew she could rely on the incessant creaking of the wheel to lead her to the giant hamster. It escaped her capacity to understand, but practically the only thing Celestina ever did was run around and around in a plastic wheel. Some nights the noise was enough to drive a cat crazy. She would jump on the bed and lick human Celeste's face until the girl woke up. Then she would hop back to the floor and go to the hamster cage, clearly indicating that human Celeste should open it and let cat Celeste put a stop to that hamster. Human Celeste never seemed to understand this. She would just give cat Celeste a pat and go back to sleep.

At least the sounds of a wheel large enough to fit the giant hamster would be easy to identify. Celeste didn't hear anything like that now, so she started on her way around the pond.

She had hardly gone more than ten paces when Ruby bounded up. The calico walked a small circle around Celeste, halting her progress. "What are you doing?" Ruby's meows vibrated with uncontrolled purring.

Ruby was a good-natured cat but Celeste didn't want her around. Although she was almost two years old, Ruby still acted like a kitten, always pouncing on things before she was ready and letting them get away. Celeste doubted Ruby could catch a pigeon with a broken wing. "Nothing. Just out for a stroll."

"A prowl you mean!" Ruby pounced on a leaf a bare two inches in front of her. "Can I come?"

If Celeste told Ruby she couldn't come, it wouldn't do any good. Either the little cat would come anyway or she would go tell all her friends and Celeste would soon be surrounded by an annoying crowd of kittens and young cats. They would make so much noise that it would be impossible to hear the giant hamster wheel.

"Okay, you can come but you have to do exactly what I say. And stay behind me."

Ruby let the dead leaf fall from her mouth so she could talk. "Thank you, thank you, thank you, Celeste." She wrinkled her pink nose and her black ears flicked in the dark. "What are we hunting?" Big yellow eyes scanned the darkness surrounding them as if the night could be full of fearsome prey.

"A hamster," Celeste said.

"What's a hamster?" Ruby asked loudly enough to scare off any hamsters that might be nearby.

"It's like a mouse, only fuzzier." She didn't want to tell Ruby she hunted a *giant* hamster. Ruby was animated enough without that. "And it doesn't have a tail."

"A mouse with no tail!" For some reason this excited Ruby. "A mouse with no tail! Just like the story." She jumped in place, her claws digging into the dirt when she landed. "Right Celeste? Just like the mice in the story."

"I don't know what story you mean," Celeste struggled to keep from growling. Ruby was making way too much noise. She would never be able to catch the giant hamster with her around.

"The three mice with no sight! You know." She slipped into a kitten's voice and began reciting a rhyme.

Three blind mice, three blind mice.

See how they run, see how they run!

They all ran after the farmer's wife.

She cut off their tails with a carving knife.

Did you ever see such a sight in your life

As three blind mice?

The rhyme was vaguely familiar. Celeste thought she had probably heard it when human Celeste was very young. She purred a little thinking of how tiny human Celeste had been back then, how cat Celeste had curled up next to her on the couch while Mother read her stories.

She decided to go along with it. "Yes, Ruby, just like that."

"Oh!" Ruby gasped. "See how they run! Little blind mice are fast. How will we ever catch them?"

Celeste tried to calm the younger cat. "I don't think the hamster will be that fast, Ruby."

"But you said *just* like. *Just like.* Just like is fast."

"Okay, not just like. Sort-of like."

Still excited, Ruby fell in beside Celeste. They managed to take several steps before Ruby broke the silence again. "How fuzzy, Celeste? Fuzzy like a teddy bear? Audrey, that's my human, has a teddy bear with big, black, button eyes. Its fur is so fuzzy you can't even see the eyes except when Audrey brushes it. And then it's just for a few minutes until the fur gets messed up again and the eyes disappear." Ruby paused for a moment. "Is that why the hamster is blind? The fur blocks its eyes?"

It took Celeste several hard thoughts to figure this out. Finally she said, "No, it's not the fur. The hamster isn't blind, it just doesn't have a tail. It's the mice in the story that are blind and I don't think it's because of their fur."

"Oh," Ruby said, clearly disappointed. "So the mouse can see us coming?"

"It's not a mouse. It's a hamster. And yes, it can see us. And hear us too, so we should be as quiet as possible."

"I can be quiet," Ruby crouched down and looked right and left with eyes as bright as flashlights. "I can be quiet as a tiger."

"Okay then," Celeste whispered and, quiet as tigers, the two cats prowled the shore of the pond.

Amazingly, Ruby was good to her word. The little feline could move like a ghost when she wanted to. Even walking right beside her, Celeste could hardly hear the other cat's paw-pats. Her own feet made sticky slurping noises in the black mud. She supposed Ruby's small size and light weight allowed her to move more silently. Celeste knew she should be happy at Ruby's stealth but she found herself angry that her pesky companion could prowl more quietly than she could.

Something bounced across the path in front of them. Celeste's reactions were lightning-fast. Instinctively, she projected the animal's course. She leaped blindly into the low weeds, claws out, teeth flashing. Of course, it wasn't the giant hamster; this animal was much too small for that. Even so, when she lifted up one paw to reveal a squirming brown mouse, Celeste sighed with disappointment.

"What is it? What is it? What is it?" Ruby bounded beside her and pushed her nose almost under Celeste's paws. "Ah! A mouse." She switched from her normal voice to that of a tiny kitten, *"Nice little mice, they make a tasty bite,"* a popular adage that mother cats teach their kittens.

"You want it?" Celeste asked.

Ruby tilted her head and looked straight into Celeste's eyes. "Want it? Want it? *Even a tasty mouse isn't allowed in the house.*"

This threw Celeste off. "No, not to take home. You can take it to your friends. Show them what a great hunter you are." Although Ruby hadn't caught the mouse herself, Celeste was reasonably sure she would be willing to take the credit.

Ruby licked her nose but didn't say anything.

"Okay, when I lift up my paw, you grab its tail."

Slowly Celeste raised her paw. She'd pressed the mouse down so hard that it had become stuck in the mud, making it difficult for the mouse to move even when Celeste's paw was completely removed. This was lucky because instead of following Celeste's advice and grabbing the mouse by the tail with her paw, Ruby made a try at catching the tiny rodent in her mouth. After a brief struggle, she raised her head with the mouse secured behind her sharp teeth. Celeste's whiskers twitched at the sight. Ruby's face was so coated in mud that the brown spot on her chin blended with the rest of her face.

"You'd better hurry to your friends. That mouse is pretty squirmy. You don't want it to get away."

Ruby's eyes opened wide. With her tail straight up in the air, she trotted off to look for her usual group of companions.

Watching the young cat disappear through the weeds, Celeste doubted Ruby would find her friends before the mouse escaped. Some cats just weren't mousers.

A high-pitched squeak caused Celeste to spin around. Her ears perked forward and she crouched low to the ground. The tip of her long black tail twitched nervously. Another squeak echoed through the dark. It wasn't a giant hamster wheel—which Celeste imagined would be lower pitched and louder—but it might be one of the tiny noises Celestina made, only greatly amplified.

She parted the weeds with her nose and looked out over the still water of the pond. At first she saw nothing. Then the reflection of the moon was disrupted by a series of ripples. Celeste followed the curve of the ripples with her eyes until she located its center. She pushed herself lower to the ground and even her tail stopped twitching. Her mind and body froze the way they had once when a large brown dog barked at her in the parking lot.

An animal that could only be the capybara sat in the center of the ring of wavelets. It didn't look anything like a hamster and "giant" did not begin to describe its size. The only part of the capybara above the water was its head–red-furred, blunt-snouted, with a tiny under-slung mouth from which hung a slimy mass of marsh algae. That head weighed as much as Celeste's whole body.

The capybara plunged its nose under the water and re-emerged with more algae. It sat eating contently and making a series of squeaks, clicks and sucking noises as it pulled the algae into its mouth.

Celeste's heart sank as she realized the impossibility of the hunt. Attacking that capybara would be no different than attacking a large dog. Only a foolish–and short-lived–cat would attempt such a feat.

In her peripheral vision she detected motion on the shore to the left of the capybara and was not surprised to see Tiger in the tall reeds, his eyes glued to the capybara. Tiger's twitching tail warned other cats not to scare off his prey. Celeste stood up. Surely Tiger wouldn't attack.

As she stood, the capybara swung its enormous head in her direction. It let out a gruff, breathy bark.

On the opposite shore, Tiger pounced, hurtling himself over the short span of water and onto the capybara's barely submerged back. His claws flashed in the moonlight.

The capybara leaped forward, crashing through the reeds, yelping and bucking. Tiger clung to its back like a drowned rat.

Without thinking, Celeste raced after them. This seemed to make the capybara run even faster. Before she knew what was happening, she was on the heels of the capybara, which were big, black and leathery. Celeste didn't dare grab for those feet. The three gigantic toes had large nails that looked like they could seriously injure a cat.

Then they were racing across the road. She heard the squeal of tires; bright lights momentarily blinded her, but she kept after Tiger and the capybara, following the universal cat credo: never abandon a hunting partner. It was what separated the cats from the dogs.

They made it safely across and headed down the embankment at breakneck speed. Tiger wailed in fear while she called encouragement to him, "Hang on Tiger! We almost have it." She knew this wasn't true but it seemed like the right thing to say.

The capybara took a hard left at the bottom, ran along the side of the ditch for a few strides and turned into a tunnel that was just capybara-sized. Unfortunately, it was not capybara-plus-cat sized and Tiger hit his head hard on the cement lip of the drainage pipe. He fell off the capybara, landing with a thud in the muddy grass.

Celeste followed so closely behind that she was forced to jump over Tiger's unmoving body and into the tunnel before she could stop. "Tiger! Tiger!" she cried as she came back to him. "Are you all right?"

Tiger didn't answer. His eyes were closed and his legs oddly bent. Celeste began licking him on the face, then the neck, then his side and back to his face. He was breathing; she could feel his side rise and fall, but he still didn't move. She started mewing his name over and over again. Lick, mew, lick, mew.

Finally Tiger's eyelids twitched and he jerked to his feet. "My head hurts," he said as Celeste breathed a deep sigh of relief.

"You hit it on the tunnel. Are you okay?"

He took a couple of steps then lay back down. "That hamster was bigger than you said."

"I know. You were very brave to attack it." She also thought he was very foolish, but she didn't say that.

"We'll need a new plan when we go after it next time."

Celeste couldn't help purring. Tiger really was brave. And loyal. He wasn't even angry with her for almost getting them killed. She was lucky to have a friend like him, although she still wished he were a little smarter.

Tiger stood up. "I can walk now, but I'm done hunting for the night. We'll try again tomorrow, right Celeste? Imagine the looks on those alley cats' faces when we bring in that hamster. They never caught anything like that." He took a hesitant step up the bank toward the road, grimaced and stepped back.

"Let's go back through the tunnel," Celeste suggested. "It's shorter that way."

"They don't call me Tiger for nothing."

Meowing agreement, Celeste walked beside Tiger into the damp darkness, letting him lean on her for support. She couldn't imagine how they would catch the capybara but if Tiger was up for a second try, then so was she. Maybe she would dream something up as she slept through the day.

* * *

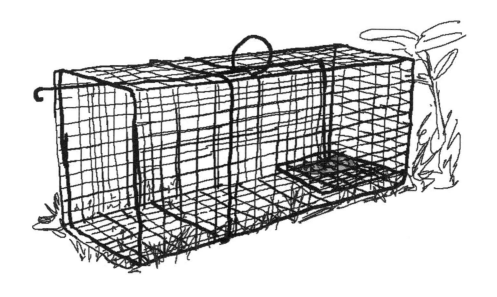

Chapter Two
How (not) to spring a trap

Her humans were already beginning to stir when Celeste pushed her nose through the cat door after walking Tiger to his apartment. She could hear the shower running and knew Mother would come to the kitchen to prepare breakfast in a few minutes. Celeste took a bite from her bowl of dry cat food, jumped on one of the dining-room chairs and curled into a ball.

She awoke when Father pulled her chair out to sit down. "Oh, there you are," he said and moved to another seat.

Celeste purred in thanks. Mother sometimes brushed Celeste off a chair but human Celeste and Father always acknowledged her right of ownership. After all, none of them ever pushed another human off their chair. Still, Mother cooked breakfast and made sure Celeste got a small portion of something tasty and good for her, so the cat never complained. A little inconvenience was fair trade.

Father reached over and clicked on the TV. He always watched the morning news during breakfast. If anything interesting happened, he would explain it to his daughter. When Mother suggested the TV should not be on during family time, Father consistently made the point that it was important for human Celeste to know about current events. "When Celeste is in high school, she is going to be the smartest one in her class because of these morning news briefs," he said. "She'll know a lot of recent history that the other kids won't."

"Fine," Mother would reply, "but is this stupid segment on disgusting foods really something you want your daughter to watch?"

Sometimes Father would agree and turn the TV off but often he came up with an interesting perspective, "It's good for Celeste to get exposure to other cultures. Just because we don't eat bats doesn't mean there's anything wrong with that. And look at the size of that thing!" Mother usually shrugged and gave up.

Human Celeste squirmed in her chair, obviously uneasy with the thought of eating a bat the size of a rabbit. Cat Celeste had the opposite reaction. She'd love to catch one of those bats, but she had no idea where Indonesia was or how to get there.

Mother put a small bowl of scrambled egg on the floor next to the counter. Celeste rose, stretched her paws in front of her, yawned and jumped down. She meandered through the maze of table, chair and human legs, rubbing against each and eliciting a scratch on the head from Father and a long pet from human Celeste, before making her way to the bowl. The warm, moist scent of the eggs made her mouth water but it was unseemly to be too eager. She arrived at the bowl with her head in the air, a gentle meow on her lips. After briefly making eye contact with Mother, she lowered her head and took a small bite. Perfect. Just the way she liked them. Celeste purred with satisfaction.

"Look at this," Father's voice raised in an uncharacteristic tone.

The TV volume increased and a woman's voice blared. "I had to slam on my brakes to avoid hitting it. It came out of nowhere. I didn't know what it was. A furry, pig-like animal with something on its back. And a cat was chasing it. And then the car behind me hit me. I heard you should never hit a pig with your car 'cause they can come right through your windshield and kill you. I don't know, maybe it wasn't a pig but that's what I thought at the time."

The video cut back to a woman newscaster talking to a man in khaki. "So you believe that was your missing capybara?" She held the microphone so he could speak into it.

"I can't be sure, of course," the man said. "It could actually have been a feral hog. There are a few of them still left in the undeveloped tracts of land in this area. But I have heard capybaras described as pig-like before."

"But capybaras aren't pigs, are they?"

"Oh no! They're rodents. Personally I think they look like giant guinea pigs. But they are so large—this one is around 120 pounds—that most people don't imagine what they're seeing is a rodent."

"120 pounds!" Mother exclaimed. "That thing weighs as much as I do."

"Well, luckily no one was hurt," the newswoman continued. "Eventually four cars were involved in the accident. John, back to you."

Father clicked the TV off and turned to Mother. "Did you see that? That looked just like the section of road in front of the apartment complex. Remember? I thought I heard an accident after we went to bed last night."

"We decided that was the neighbor's TV. And you know all the roads around here look the same."

"Daddy, is the giant hamster living here? Can we see it?"

"It's not living here," Mother answered in a stern voice.

"Get your homework done and we'll go look for it when I get off work," Father told human Celeste. "We'll take our bikes and go around the block, okay?"

Human Celeste's head bobbed up and down.

"You won't see anything," Mother said.

"Maybe not but we can try, and the exercise will be good for us. Want to come?"

Mother laughed. "You two are crazy."

"Come with us!" human Celeste pleaded.

"Oh, all right. But you have to get your homework done first. Now go brush your hair and get ready for school."

Human Celeste scurried off to the bathroom. Mother was constantly telling her to brush her hair and her hair always needed brushing. It was long and straight and nearly as black as cat Celeste's fur. She usually had it tied with little purple or pink bows and these were what kept getting messed up. Sometimes human Celeste would capture cat Celeste and hold her tightly while clipping a bow to her ear or her tail. For this reason, cat Celeste decided to sneak back into the bedroom and go to sleep.

Celeste woke several times during the day even though the apartment was empty. Generally she would do a leisurely walk-around, making sure she was aware of everything that happened within the confines of her home. She finished the bowl of scrambled egg for lunch and ate dried food for her afternoon snack.

The two adult humans took turns getting off work early and picking up their daughter at after-school care. Today Mother and human Celeste arrived home at exactly 4:17 pm. Cat Celeste noted the time carefully. She often did things during the day that she felt no human should see, so she liked to keep track of everyone's schedules.

Human Celeste went straight to her room and started her homework. Cat Celeste curled up on the windowsill beside the desk, purring softly. Occasionally human Celeste put down her pencil for a moment to stroke her cat. The sun warmed Celeste's fur and things were nearly perfect when Mother brought human Celeste a peanut butter-and-jelly sandwich and cat Celeste a tidbit of chicken from the night's dinner.

Human Celeste picked up the sandwich and took a dainty bite out of one corner. With her mouth full of peanut butter she said, "Two more math problems and I'm finished with my homework. When is Daddy coming home?"

"Should be any time now. Let me look over your work."

The two humans rustled papers and books while Celeste went back to sleep. The late-afternoon sun warmed her dark fur like a blanket. She didn't bother to open her eyes when she heard Father's voice in the living room. Soon she had the apartment to herself. Celeste took advantage of her solitude by sleeping especially soundly.

She woke to the front door barging open and the shrill, excited voice of human Celeste. "But do you think they'll catch her, Daddy? I don't want them to. I want Caplynn Rose to live in the field forever."

"Well, I don't know, Celeste. That man seemed like he knew what he was doing. If the capybara likes corn-on-the-cob as much as he said, then she'll go in one of the traps he set and he'll catch her."

"Really, Celeste." Mother's voice was soothing but firm. "You have to think about what's best for the animal. Mr. Levan told you they're from the tropics. They can't live here. How would you feel if the poor thing froze to death during the winter?"

Cat Celeste hopped down from the windowsill and made her way to the living room as quickly as she could without appearing to hurry. As a cat she was always careful about this, even if no one was watching. She walked to her bowl and pretended to eat while listening closely to the conversation.

"But it doesn't get that cold here," human Celeste protested. "It never even snows. And Caplynn Rose might be able to find some place warm to sleep at night. Maybe in the Jacuzzi."

"Oh! I can just imagine that," Mother said. "A 120- pound giant hamster lounging in the apartment complex Jacuzzi during the cold winter nights."

"They turn the Jacuzzi off during the winter," Father said. "Remember? The pool and the Jacuzzi close at the end of October."

Human Celeste slumped down on the couch.

Father sat next to her. "Well, it was nice of Mr. Levan to talk to us. And we'll take him up on his offer to visit Caplynn Rose after he catches her again. That'll be fun, won't it?"

"I guess." Human Celeste did not sound happy.

"I know. Not as fun as having a capybara live here, but still pretty fun."

Cat Celeste meowed loudly to break up the conversation. She wanted to hear about the giant hamster and how to catch it but this discussion of how great it would be to have one living near the apartment disturbed her. Humans often said cats were hard to understand but conversations like this left cat Celeste so confused she felt dizzy. Celestina was bad enough, but at least she was confined to a cage. A monstrous hamster living wild in the field could not be something anyone would desire.

"Now go wash up for dinner," Father said.

Human Celeste shuffled to the hall. "I wish Caplynn Rose could live with us." She whined just loudly enough for her parents to hear.

"If wishes were horses beggars would ride," Father said sternly. "You don't get everything you want, Celeste, and whining about it doesn't make it better."

"I do wish we could see it," Mother said. "I can't believe it's as friendly as Mr. Levan described. It sounds just like a dog."

"If it were really just like a dog, he wouldn't be having so much trouble catching it. A dog would come when he called."

Mother nodded. "What did he say the Rose part of her name stands for?"

"It's really R-O-U-S, Rodent Of Unusual Size. It's from that movie, The Princess Bride."

"Well, he got that right. At 120 pounds that animal is a rodent of unusual size! I'm glad it's an herbivore or I'd be afraid the local dogs would start disappearing."

Father laughed. Then, in a serious voice, he added, "Do you think we need to keep Celeste inside? She's not a very big cat. What would happen if she ran into that thing?"

Celeste stopped breathing. She did not want to be locked up. Her humans did not confine her very often and she usually made them regret it by clawing the furniture or tearing up some favored item. She couldn't believe they would risk her ire over a giant hamster.

"She'll be fine," Mother replied. "Celeste may be small but she can take care of herself."

With the threat of imprisonment fresh in her mind, Celeste took a few bites of cat food and headed for the door. The sun had just set. It was still too light to hunt but she couldn't risk her humans' fickle whims when it came to latching the cat door. She had to go while the going was good.

She bounded down the concrete steps to the first floor landing, then turned left toward Tiger's apartment.

"Celeste." A deep, purring voice caught her attention.

Celeste turned to see Pumpkin sitting on the fence. He was a big cat, orange as his namesake, with darker orange circles on his sides and four white paws. He had only half of his left ear, the other half having been shredded during a terrible fight in his youth. A long, hairless scar traced down one hind leg, trophy of another fight.

Pumpkin jumped from the fence and strode toward her. Celeste stood perfectly still. She wasn't afraid of Pumpkin—or at least she told herself she wasn't—but there was no point upsetting the big cat unnecessarily. "Hi, Pumpkin," she said in her sweetest voice.

"Going hunting again tonight?" Pumpkin's voice was so low she could feel it vibrate through her body.

"I was just going to check on Tiger."

"Ah," Pumpkin sat on his haunches.

Since he kept looking at her, Celeste kept talking. "He got hurt last night. I just wanted to make sure he's okay."

"Hurt? How?"

Celeste did not want to tell Pumpkin about the giant hamster. As the largest, oldest and strongest cat in the neighborhood, Pumpkin would claim the hamster for his own. "He hit his head."

"Really?"

"He wasn't watching where he was going. You know how Tiger is." Celeste licked her paw in an attempt to act unconcerned.

"Celeste! Celeste! Celeste!"

Celeste put her paw down and saw Ruby squirming out from under a hedge. The little spotted cat slid up next to Pumpkin and would have rubbed against him if the larger cat had not hissed a warning.

"Celeste, are we going hunting again tonight? That was fun. Did you catch the no-tail mouse?"

"No-tail mouse?" Pumpkin asked.

Oblivious to the tension between the older cats, Ruby chanted, *"No-tail mouse with fuzzy fur. Celeste calls it a hamster!"*

Pumpkin blinked. "A hamster? You were out hunting a hamster last night when Tiger got hurt?"

Celeste nodded.

Pumpkin stood and walked back toward the fence. He crouched, coiling his muscular frame, and easily jumped to the narrow board that ran along the top. Looking back down at Celeste, he meowed a laugh. "Let me know when you catch it, if you can. Don't let it hurt you too badly."

The other tom cats sitting on the fence all laughed at his joke. Celeste felt her hair bristling. Let them laugh now. When she brought the capybara in, it would be her turn to laugh. She turned her back to them and started off through the parking lot toward Tiger's apartment.

"Are we going hunting again, Celeste? Are we?" Ruby padded alongside her, carelessly splashing through puddles.

Flicking her ears in annoyance, Celeste accepted that Ruby would tag along for another night of prowling. "First we have to check on Tiger."

They met the big cat as he descended the last flight of the stairs of his apartment building.

"Are you okay?" Celeste asked.

The tabby stretched his large paws out before him and arched his back so that every muscle strained. "A little stiff but I'm fine." He gingerly descended the final few steps. "What's the plan for tonight?"

"Yes, yes," Ruby chimed. "What's our plan tonight, Celeste? Are we going around the pond again? I liked that."

"That plan didn't work, Ruby. We need a new plan. I have one but it's a little hard to explain." Celeste started walking and the others followed her. As they hurried along, Celeste gave her companions a brief outline of her plan. Luckily they didn't ask for any details. Some cats were all about planning, preparing and pouncing, the "Three P's" as her mother used to say. Celeste knew herself to be more of the spontaneous, live-in-the-moment kind of cat. She was really only good at the last of the Three P's.

Celeste led her companions through the metal bars of the fence. Along the road or where it could be seen by prospective tenants, the fence was black wrought-iron; everywhere else it was a wooden privacy fence. This worked out well for the cats since the wrought-iron part allowed easy access in and out of the complex while the wooden part provided an excellent singing stage. Since the pond was near the road, the section of fence closest to it was made of narrow iron bars spaced just widely enough for a cat to slide between.

"So now we need to find one of the traps," Celeste told Ruby and Tiger as they looked out over the pond. The sun had set and the western horizon still glowed. In the reflected light, the water looked blood-red. "Tiger, you take the pond. Ruby, you search the field as far back as the end of the complex. I'll take the road verge. Whoever finds a trap, call out and the other cats will come to you. Okay?"

Both cats nodded but before her head had even stopped moving, Ruby popped a question, "What's a road verge, Celeste? Isn't that dangerous? Audrey always yells at me when I go near the road. Are you going to go near the road? Is that safe?"

"The verge is just the edge of the road but not the road itself. The humans wouldn't put a trap *on* the road but they might put one next to it. Yes, it is dangerous, that's why I'm taking that job for myself. I'll be very careful."

Even though Ruby nodded again, she didn't seem convinced. "But I'm careful and Audrey still won't let me go near the road. And Mother won't let Audrey go near the road. It's not safe."

Celeste didn't like the younger cat questioning her judgment but she understood her concern. "I promise I'll be careful. Now let's go. We have a giant hamster to catch."

"A *giant* hamster? Giant? Giant?" Ruby had turned into a bouncing ball of fur. "You didn't say *giant* hamster before. Is it a monster? Is it scary? Is it dangerous? How big is it?"

"It's pretty big," Tiger said. "As big as that dog that lives in apartment 312."

Ruby's eyes glowed in the dark. "Dogs eat cats. Do giant hamsters eat cats?"

"The hamster isn't dangerous. It's big but it's still just a hamster. Cats eat hamsters, not the other way around."

This did not reassure Ruby. She stood with her back slightly arched and her multi-colored hair standing on end.

"It will be fine," Celeste said. "Let's get going. We need to find one of the traps."

The three cats separated, Tiger heading for the pond, Ruby for the field and Celeste toward the road. Except that, after just a few steps, Celeste found Ruby back at her side.

"Can I go with you?" Ruby asked.

"I need you to search the field."

Brushing against her and purring loudly, Ruby said, "I don't want to go by myself. Let's look at the road first then we can both go to the field."

"You're not afraid of a hamster, are you?"

"No," Ruby said slowly. "But I am afraid of a giant hamster. A giant hamster might eat a cat. The giant hamster hurt Tiger last night, didn't it? I am smaller than Tiger."

Celeste sighed. There didn't seem to be any point to arguing with Ruby. The young cat's ears twitched nervously and she pushed herself much closer to Celeste than was comfortable. Mr. Levan probably wouldn't put traps in the field anyway since there was no water out there. She had told Ruby to search there just to keep her busy.

"All right, then, you can come with me. But be quiet."

The two cats walked delicately through the tall grass down into the gully next to the road. Sticky mud lined the bottom and Celeste did not like getting her feet dirty. Ruby didn't mind at all; she trotted easily through the weeds and muck.

"What will a trap look like?" Ruby asked after a few minutes.

"Metal, I think. Big enough for one of us to crawl into. And it will have an ear of corn in it."

"Yes, yes. We take the corn and catch the giant hamster ourselves. No traps, just sharp claws and teeth." Ruby bared her teeth menacingly.

"Right."

"Three cats against one giant hamster."

"Don't worry," Celeste said. "Tiger almost caught it by himself last night. The giant hamster is no match for the three of us."

"Right," Ruby agreed.

Moonlight glinted off something ahead of them and Celeste froze.

Ruby took another step and then flattened herself against the ground. She turned her head and looked back at Celeste. "What is it?"

"There's something up ahead."

"Is it a trap?"

Sniffing the air and perking her ears forward, Celeste did not detect any danger. "I think so." She advanced slowly, skirting around to the side. She wanted to get a good view of the thing before she approached it.

Ruby followed behind, stepping in her pawprints. "Can it hurt us?"

"It's supposed to catch the giant hamster without hurting it, so it shouldn't hurt us either." The trap sat in a low place in the grass, its heavy base sunk into the mud. The visible part was a long rectangular box made of metal mesh. One of the short ends of the box was open. At the opposite end sat an ear of uncooked corn. The trap really didn't look dangerous.

Celeste sat down in front of the open end and called into the light wind that stirred the grass. In a moment she heard Tiger's answer. He wasn't far.

While she waited, Celeste eyed the trap trying to figure out how it worked.

"Can't we just go in and get the corn? It looks easy." Ruby went right up to the front of the trap and put one paw inside.

"Don't do that. We don't know how it works. You could get stuck in there."

Ruby jumped back, the hair rising along her back. "Maybe it only catches hamsters. Maybe it can't catch cats."

Humans were clever. It was possible they could build a trap specific to giant hamsters, but Celeste wasn't sure. "Let's wait for Tiger."

In a minute they heard a soft meow. When Celeste answered, the orange tabby slid out of the tall grass behind them. "So that's a trap?"

"I think the door closes when an animal lifts up the corn," Celeste said. "One of us should go inside and take the bait while someone else stands at the front and keeps the gate from swinging down."

"I can't go inside," Ruby said, crouching down in the grass. "I don't' want to get stuck in there."

"That's okay," Celeste said. "I'll go in. Tiger can hold the gate up. You stand guard."

"Good. Good." Ruby stood up, swiveling her head around as if guarding them already.

"What do I do?" Tiger asked.

"You walk right beside me as I go in but stop in the entrance. If the gate starts to swing closed, arch your back and hold it up. I'll get the corn and then we'll both get out. After that it doesn't matter if the trap closes."

Ruby had already started pacing a small circle around the other cats and the trap. Celeste waited until Ruby was on the far side before she placed her first paw into the trap. Tiger's larger paw fell just beside hers. Nothing happened and Celeste breathed easier. Another step and the two cats had their heads in the trap. Celeste could see Ruby through the metal mesh. She and Tiger took a third step. Now their shoulders were inside the trap and still nothing had happened. Two more steps and Celeste was completely inside, only Tiger's tail flicked in the open air.

"You wait here," Celeste whispered.

"Good luck," Tiger responded, already arching his back.

Celeste stepped forward cautiously, placing one paw in front of the other and then shifting her weight forward. She didn't like the feel of the trap. The breeze that rustled the grass had no effect on these metal bars.

Moving forward, Celeste noticed that the cob of corn lay on a special section of the floor of the trap. This part was slightly raised. She avoided stepping onto it. She picked the corn up with her teeth. The cob was heavier than she imagined and the corn leaked a sharp-tasting juice into her mouth. It was hard not to spit it out.

Celeste perked her ears. A musical clicking sound echoed through the dark and then stopped. She stepped backward toward Tiger and the exit. The clicking started up again, louder and closer. Celeste jumped and dropped the corn, which rattled against the metal of the cage. A squeak pierced the dark along with the sound of mud sucking at paws moving through the marshy road edge. The footsteps were getting closer.

Out of the corner of her eye, Celeste saw Ruby, hair standing on end, race toward Tiger and the front of the trap. Celeste tried to turn to brace Tiger against the impact but the trap was narrow and one of her hind paws caught on the wire. Ruby crashed into Tiger. The two of them tumbled forward, pushing against Celeste, who was already off-balance. Celeste fell on her side, toward the back of the trap. The metal floor gave beneath her. Above her a silver bar slid. The mechanism of the trap became clear. When the false floor under the corn was pressed down, it moved a bar on the roof that held the door open.

The trap door slammed down on Ruby. The little cat screamed as she was pushed hard against Tiger. She kept crying, her plaintive mews muffled by Tiger's fur.

A shape moved outside the trap and Celeste almost snapped her neck trying to follow it. She heard more of the musical clicks as the giant hamster circled the trap. It poked its large flat nose at her and squeaked. Two big white teeth showed through its split upper lip. Celeste shoved the end of the corncob out through the mesh. The capybara grabbed it and pulled it through. Then it walked off into the dark, the cob hanging out of its mouth.

"Ouch! Help me. My tail is stuck. Ouch!" Ruby must have gotten her face out of Tiger's fur because her voice was loud and clear. "Help me!"

"Hold still," Tiger said. "When I push against the door, pull your tail out." The big cat pushed as hard as he could but the door didn't move. "It's not working. Celeste! What should we do?" He turned his big yellow eyes to Celeste. Tiger was a tough character but he couldn't stand to see other cats suffer.

"We have to undo what we did that made the door close in the first place," Celeste reasoned aloud. "Pushing the raised floor down tripped the mechanism. If we can pick it up, the door should lift." She grabbed the metal mesh with her teeth but couldn't budge it.

Tiger came over to help and the two of them managed to get the trap door open a half inch. Ruby pulled her tail through but continued to mew plaintively. "I think it's broken. I don't want to be one of those cats with a kinked tail."

Tiger didn't say anything but Celeste knew his feelings were hurt. The last two inches of his tail had been kinked since kittenhood. He tucked it around his feet and sat in the center of the trap.

The capybara must have finished its corn because it came back. It walked all around, squeaking and chirping like a bird, staring at the three captives. "Eep, eep, eep," it said over and over.

Celeste didn't know what to do and didn't have much time to think of it before Tiger started making imitations of the sound. The capybara came up to the trap and pushed its nose against it. Tiger took a step and leaned his nose toward the capybara's.

"Tiger, stop! That is not safe. You don't know anything about that animal. It has enormous teeth. It could bite your nose off," Celeste warned.

The other cat looked doubtful but sat back down.

In a minute the capybara wandered off. They could hear its quiet clicking over the sound of Ruby's moans.

* * *

Chapter Three
How (not) to win a dogfight

The three cats sat cramped and cold through the long night. After an hour Ruby stopped mewing, more because she was tired than because her tail had stopped hurting. Toward dawn, a damp, cold fog rose from the moist ground. The cats puffed out their fur to keep warm but soon silver droplets of water sparkled on every hair and the tip of each whisker.

In the first light, the capybara returned. It was thoroughly wet and covered with tiny green seed pods that had rubbed off the damp grass and stuck to the animal's stiff coat. Even though its fur lay flat against its body, in places Celeste could see pink skin between the reddish-brown hairs.

It was cramped in the trap and difficult to move. Ruby jostled the others and cried as she struggled to turn to face the capybara. She hissed when she saw it and backed farther into Tiger, who pushed into Celeste.

The capybara was not frightened. It looked at them through the wire mesh, took a bite of grass, and looked at them some more. In the light, it appeared even more frightening and fierce-looking. The tiny mouse ears that sprouted from its enormous head flicked rapidly. Its rectangular snout had small nostrils nearly all the way on top. Its upper lip was split like a rabbit's and, through the slit, Celeste saw two sharp, white teeth, longer than even her longest claw.

It came over and nosed through the grass, picking up kernels of corn that had scraped off when Celeste pushed the cob through the wires. Its tiny pink tongue curled around each yellow tidbit as its lips twisted and grabbed at the morsel.

Upon close examination, Celeste determined that the capybara did not look anything like a hamster. Even Celestina was a beautiful, graceful creature compared to this monster. At least Celestina's downy fur completely covered her pudgy little body. And the dwarf hamster's front paws were almost as useful as human hands. The front paws of the capybara had four toes, each of which was tipped with a blunt, black nail that looked like a pig's hoof. Between the toes stretched a web of skin that made the feet even more hideous. But the front feet were beautiful in comparison to the back, which had only three enormous, black, leathery toes and looked like grotesquely deformed duck feet.

"Make it go away," Ruby whimpered, her voice muffled by Tiger's fur.

Celeste turned her attention to her companions. Tiger sat bravely watching the capybara but fear showed in his eyes. Ruby had pushed herself underneath him, and looked out between his forelegs as if they were the columns of a great house.

Although the capybara frightened Celeste as much as it did the others, she could see they were looking to her for leadership. She turned to the monster and raised one paw, claws extended.

The apparition lifted its head and looked at her out of its great, black eyes.

She swiped at it and hissed as fiercely as she could.

The capybara gave a loud bark that sounded like a dog with a bad cough, spun on its enormous black heels and crashed away through the grass, sending droplets of dew everywhere, including onto Celeste's nose.

The other cats scrunched closer to her, Tiger on her left and Ruby on the right. The three of them formed a solid wall facing out in the direction of the vanquished capybara.

Just then they heard the sound of tires on the gravel road shoulder behind them. A car door opened and closed, and human footsteps shuffled through the damp grass.

All three of them tried to turn at once, pushing and shoving against each other and the walls of the trap. With no understanding of how it happened, Celeste found Tiger's back under her stomach and her two front paws planted on Ruby's head. She dug her claws in to keep from falling as Tiger squirmed out from under her. Ruby howled and managed to draw her head back, causing Celeste to crash to the floor, landing on her back.

"Well, what have we here?" a man's voice boomed.

Celeste could see his dark face with black eyes behind wireless glasses peering down at her. His lips parted in a slender smile. "Three cats? Three wet cats where there should be one capybara." He straightened and laughed. "Now there's something I wasn't expecting."

He moved around to the front of the trap, taking careful steps in the mud and talking all the while. "And what would three cats be doing in a trap baited with a cob of fresh corn? I might have expected it if I'd been using catnip. But, even then, *three*?" His voice rose in pitch at his astonishment. "Three cats in one trap. I couldn't have done any better if I'd been going after cats."

He knelt down and began fiddling with the trap door. "I guess I'm just going to have to let you go, but I suspect you've been giving me some trouble. Seeing the three of you here reminds me of that woman's story. A cat on the back of old Caplynn Rous and another chasing her when she crossed the road." He held the trap door partly open, eyeing them suspiciously. "You wouldn't be them same cats now, would you?" He shook his head and rubbed his chin with one hand. "Well, there are three of you and only two in that woman's story, so at least one of you is innocent." He opened the trap door wide.

"Run!" Celeste cried to Tiger and Ruby. "Run before he changes his mind."

Tiger shot out first, following the path of parted grass left by the capybara. Ruby came behind, howling from the pain of her tail as she hit it on the wire top of the cage in her hurry. Celeste was the last to go and she felt the man's hand on her back as she made her escape, plunging wildly behind her companions, not caring what direction they took.

"Now don't make me regret this," the man called after them. "I like cats but I'll take the lot of you to the pound if I catch you again."

It was late in the morning and the parking lot was nearly empty as the cats made their way back to the apartment complex.

"What is Audrey going to say about my beautiful tail?" Ruby whimpered. "She always loved my tail."

"Don't worry about it," Celeste told her. "Probably Audrey won't even notice." But she knew this wasn't true. Ruby's tail had more than just a kink in it. The last inch or so dangled lifelessly. Celeste cringed inside. The injury to Ruby's tail was in some way her fault. If she hadn't been so bent on catching the giant hamster–capybara–then none of this would have happened and Ruby's tail would be straight.

"A kink in the tail's not such a bad thing," Tiger said. "I've had one as long as I can remember and it's never caused me any trouble."

Ruby meowed softly, "But you're a tom. It makes you look rugged and handsome." Ruby turned to examine her own tail. "Look at it! My beautiful tail." She sobbed a series of plaintive meows.

"Well," Celeste said, "I remember when human Celeste's Uncle Aaron broke his arm and they put a cast on it to hold it still. After a long time they took the cast off and his arm was fine. They could do that with your tail."

Ruby looked doubtful. "His arm was fine? No kink? And he could move it like his other arm?"

"You couldn't even tell he broke it."

"Do you think a cast would work on my tail?" Ruby looked first at Celeste and then at Tiger, then back to Celeste. The two cats nodded in unison.

"I remember a long time back," Tiger began, "there was a little girl with a broken leg in apartment 527. That's on the second floor so her parents had to carry her up and down the stairs every day to go to school. When they took the cast off, she could walk up the stairs by herself. I don't see why it wouldn't work on tails."

"Hurt yourself, have you?" A deep meow oozed from beneath a nearby car. Celeste saw Phukat, a slinky Siamese, rise gracefully to his chocolate-brown paws. "And where's the hamster?"

Celeste felt the hair on her back stand on end. She willed it to lie flat. "Did Pumpkin send you to spy on us?"

Phukat sat down beside the front tire, the light tan of his coat brightly contrasted against the black wheel. He licked his paw and then rubbed it over his ear. "I'm not spying," he said. "Just curious. No one expects Ruby to be able to catch a fly, but the two of you..." He licked his paw again. "The two of you should be more than a match for a hamster." He put his paw down and turned his cold blue eyes to them. "So where is it?"

"It got away," Tiger stated.

"And bit Ruby's tail as it ran? That looks like a pretty bad break."

Ruby pushed herself against Tiger for support. "It's nothing," she squeaked.

Phukat purred his amusement. "Nothing for a big, brave cat like Tiger. Or even Celeste. But it's quite something for a pretty little cat like you, Ruby. And it doesn't look like an injury a hamster could cause."

"She got her tail caught in a trap down by the pond. We didn't even see the hamster."

Phukat's ears went back and his whiskers raised in a questioning look.

Just then Tiger sprang forward, landing between Celeste and Phukat. "Listen!"

All the cats froze. Celeste's skin prickled. "Get under the cars!" she called to Ruby and Tiger. She dove forward, nearly crashing into Phukat as the Siamese made a similar move. Celeste spun around, hissing, her ears pinned against her head.

A long, brown snout with gapping jaws and jagged teeth pushed under the car. The big dog could not get more than the tip of its nose underneath the little sports car where they had taken refuge. Celeste lashed out, her claws fully deployed, and whacked it across the nose. Its teeth snapped back but missed her paw.

"Merrow!"

Celeste turned to see Ruby and Tiger fighting a pair of wiener dogs. As usual, the nasty animals traveled in packs and coordinated their actions. The small dogs could fit under the car and were trying to drive the cats into the open where their larger companion could get them.

"We can't stay here," Phukat hissed at Celeste. Among cats, even the worst of enemies were comrades against dogs.

"My apartment is right there," Celeste yelled to be heard over the din of barking. "On the second floor. There's an open cat door." She clawed at the big dog again. "If we run, we should be able to make it. Dogs can't climb stairs very fast."

Phukat turned to help Tiger and Ruby combat the stout little dogs. They had divided, one attacking from the front of the car and the other making repeated jabs from the area near the tailpipe.

"We can't all go at once," Celeste called to the battling cats. "Tiger and Ruby go first. Phukat and I will keep the dogs occupied."

"Okay," Tiger and Ruby said together.

Phukat jumped forward, whacking one of the dachshunds hard across the nose. The dog scuttled back, yelping. "Go!" he called.

Ruby and Tiger leaped forward as one. Celeste caught only a glimpse of their escape but she was glad to see Tiger let Ruby take the lead. The large dog lifted its head. In the moment of hesitation before the dog took off after her fleeing friends, Celeste attacked. She rushed out from under the car and grabbed the dog's snout with her claws and teeth. Immediately the animal turned its attention back to her, shaking its head and throwing

Celeste to the ground. She felt its teeth rake her hind leg as she slid back to safety.

Now two cats fought three dogs. Celeste retreated until she and Phukat stood nose-to-tail under the center of the car. The dogs gave them no opening. Celeste could feel a trickle of blood run down her leg.

"Go now!" Phukat called, springing out from under the car. Celeste didn't have time to think, and no choice but to follow. In a moment she understood Phukat's plan. The two cats just barely beat a car pulling into the empty parking space next to them. The big dog and one of the dachshunds had to run around it, yapping and barking as they raced to catch the cats.

The second dachshund nearly chomped Celeste's tail as they bounded up the stairs. The long-bodied canine proved surprisingly agile. Celeste darted through the cat door with the dog only a step behind.

Celeste felt the rush of air as the small dog pushed through the door behind her. She raced across the room without looking back and jumped onto the couch. The little dog launched itself at her, snapping as she leaped from the couch to the kitchen counter.

Her feet slid on the slick surface and she plunged into the sink, bumping into the faucet and knocking around the soaking breakfast dishes. She jumped out of the water in time to see the second wiener dog push its way through the cat door.

"Help! Help!" Ruby called.

Celeste skid across the counter. She spotted the little cat trapped on a dining-room chair that was pushed under the table. One of the dogs had its front paws on the chair and was snapping at her.

Tiger raced under the table, taking one quick swipe at the dog's tail and eliciting a high-pitched yelp. He bounded to a breakfast stool and leaned down to jab at his pursuer's nose. When the second wiener dog joined in, Tiger retreated to the counter.

Ruby made a dash for the bookshelf. She landed on the top shelf, knocking a couple of books to the floor.

Celeste slid across the wet countertop. She jumped onto the kitchen linoleum and landed in a small puddle of dishwater, causing her feet to splay out under her. She regained solid footing when she reached the carpet and gathered herself up in time to jump over the two dogs and head for the cat door.

"Tiger!" she called without turning her head or slacking her pace. "When I come back, slam the flap down behind me and hold it closed!" Years of experience allowed her to flip the cat door open without losing momentum. Her paws hit the concrete floor of the breezeway. Four long, brown legs surrounded her like pillars. Celeste scrunched her body low to the ground and shot between the dog's hind legs.

She managed one quick look over her shoulder as she reached the stairwell. The two wiener dogs and the brown dog were a tangle of legs that collapsed in a heap as she watched. Celeste made the landing and two more jumps of three steps each before she heard the clatter of dog claws at the top of the stairs.

When she reached ground level, Celeste whipped around the corner of the building. She let the dogs gain on her, she needed them close enough that they wouldn't decide to forget about her and go back for the other cats. Then she rocketed up the opposite staircase and down the breezeway. The smaller of the wiener dogs had just reached the breezeway when Celeste pushed through the cat door.

Tiger shouldered her out of the way as he pushed the door closed. Slam! Tiger bumped off the door with the force of the impact and Celeste rushed to help.

"Yap, yap, yap, yap, yap!"

An apartment door creaked open. "Go on! Get out of here!" A man's voice yelled. Heavy stomping. The barks grew more distant. "Stupid dogs." A door slammed.

Everything became still. Celeste couldn't hear anything over the pounding of her heart. Slowly the sounds of the apartment building reasserted themselves. Water was running somewhere.

"Where is Phukat?" Celeste asked.

"He ran out right after the dogs left."

Celeste trotted to her favorite spot at the window. In the parking lot she saw the big brown dog being dragged away by its collar. The dachshunds were nowhere to be seen. Phukat lay on his side on the hood of a green SUV, his head tilted so he could clean his paws.

"Do you see anything?" Tiger said from the floor.

"He's fine," Celeste replied, shaking her ears. Her hind leg throbbed as she slid back to the carpet next to Tiger.

"Meow," Ruby murmured.

"We'd better get Ruby home," Celeste said. "Her humans will know how to put a cast on her tail. It might be important to do it quickly."

She started to walk toward the door but stumbled when she put full weight on her hurt leg.

"I can take her home," Tiger said. The big cat had come out of the fight without a scratch. "You should wait here for your humans. They might want to do something with your leg."

Celeste sat down and twisted her body so she could lick her wound. It wasn't anything serious. She was just tired and stiff. But she agreed to Tiger's suggestion. When the others had gone, she climbed back to her favorite spot of morning sun and quickly fell asleep.

* * *

Knock! Knock!

Celeste nearly jumped out of her fur.

"Monica? Philip? Are you in there?" a woman's voice called through the door.

It was quiet except for the normal apartment sounds—cars in the parking lot, the pounding rhythm of music, and water running in a sink—while the woman waited for a response.

"Monica? There's water coming through my ceiling." The woman was yelling now. "Please open up or I'm going to have to get the manager."

The rubber flap of the cat door stirred. Celeste realized the woman must be trying to look in. Her leg had stiffened while she slept so she didn't get up. After a moment she heard the woman walk away.

Just as Celeste was starting to doze off again, she heard two pairs of human feet climbing the stairs.

"I'm sure it's nothing," a young man said. "They probably just left the water on. You'd be surprised how often that happens."

"I hope so," the familiar woman's voice replied. "It doesn't seem like something Monica or Philip would do."

Celeste perked her ears but didn't stir from her location. She heard a key turn in the lock and then the door opening.

Heavy footsteps strode purposefully across the floor. They squished in the carpet as they got closer to the kitchen and then actually splashed when they reached the hard vinyl.

"Looks like they left the kitchen sink running," the man said. "What a mess."

Celeste sat up, suddenly awake. The sound of running water had been coming from her own apartment! Her mind raced through the fight with the two dachshunds. She remembered falling in the sink. Like all cats, she hated the water. Getting out had been her only objective. Now she realized she had used the faucet for a foothold. She had turned the water on and it had been running ever since.

"Can you check the rest of the apartment?" The woman said. "There are a couple of broken dishes. That doesn't seem right. What if they're hurt and lying in one of the other rooms too weak to move?"

The man sighed but Celeste heard him open the door to the master bedroom, then the bath. Then a curly-haired, dark-eyed face poked into her room. She didn't move.

"There's a cat in here. Maybe that's what you heard earlier. It doesn't look hurt or anything...oh wait, there's a cut on its leg."

The woman came up behind the man and Celeste saw it was Kristina Colorado, the downstairs neighbor.

"That's their cat," she said. She came in the room and walked up to Celeste.

Kristina sometimes left a bowl of milk out for the neighborhood cats so Celeste allowed herself to be petted. Kristina was a nice woman but she didn't understand that you must always stroke a cat from front to back, in the direction of their hair, and not the other way around.

"Are you okay, kitty?" Kristina asked, peering at Celeste's wounded leg. When she made a move to touch it, Celeste pulled away. "I'm sorry, girl. I just want to see if it's serious."

Celeste purred a little to reassure Kristina but tucked the bad leg under her so there could be no misunderstanding.

Kristina sighed. Then both humans walked out of the room and finished checking the house.

"There doesn't seem to be a problem except for leaving the water on and a few broken dishes," the man said. "I have to go back to the office and get their contact numbers but I'll give them a call and have them come clean this up."

"Then that's it? What about my place?"

"Let me call the residents, then I'll come over and assess the damage to your apartment."

Their voices became too muffled for Celeste to hear as the door closed and the lock turned.

Celeste was exhausted from the events of the night and morning. She'd hardly gotten so much as a catnap while trapped in the cage. Like most cats, she didn't like to stay awake for long periods. As the lock clicked, Celeste lay her head down and promptly fell asleep.

The sound of a key in the lock woke her. She recognized the way Father turned the handle and the sound of his footsteps in the entry. She hopped down from her perch, relieved that the leg felt much better already. She watched from behind the half-closed door.

Father didn't look or sound angry. He began picking up the dishes that had fallen from the counter and broken. When he was done with that, Celeste watched him mop the kitchen floor. It took him a long time and each time he finished, more water seeped out of the carpet and onto the vinyl.

Father stood straight and wiped his brow with his sleeve. "That's a lot of water," he muttered to himself. "I can't believe Monica left the sink on."

After that he opened the front door, the door to their small balcony and the window in the living room. He left the apartment for a few minutes. When he came back he was carrying two large fans. He set one up at the front door and one at the door to the balcony. When they were both on, a strong breeze blew through the apartment.

Celeste decided it was safe to come out after Father got the towels out of the bathroom and began to use them to sop up the water in the carpet. She brushed against his arm as he pushed a wet towel.

Father stopped what he was doing, sat back on his heels and scratched Celeste behind the ears. "Just look at this mess, will you? If only you could have turned the water off." He stroked her back as he spoke. "But cat paws can't really do that, can they girl?" He picked her up and took one of her front paws in his hand. "Good for catching mice but not much else." He set her back down. "Well, I'm sure you would have if you could. Good cat." He went back to his work.

Celeste felt a tight little knot in her belly. She'd made a mistake and she didn't mind living up to it but she had no way to communicate this to her human family.

She decided to leave Father alone and go get some food. That required walking over the wettest areas of the carpet. Celeste picked her feet up daintily, shaking the water off with each step until she reached the kitchen. The vinyl floor was damp but not enough to get her wet.

When she got to her dry food bowl she found the food was not dry. Water had splashed as it cascaded from the sink, making her food soggy. Not wanting to disturb Father, she used her paw to scoop the wet stuff onto the floor. It took several pawfulls to clear out enough to allow the tall dispenser to refill the bowl at the bottom with dry food. She took three bites, decided she was full and went back to her room for a nap.

* * *

Chapter Four
How (not) to console a friend

That night Celeste was too tired to go hunting. The apartment was cold because Father insisted on keeping the doors open and the fans on, even during dinner. Human Celeste gave cat Celeste a tidbit of her chicken and Mother and Father gave her nothing. They didn't talk much after their argument when Mother came home with human Celeste.

"You left the water on in the sink," Father said matter-of-factly when Mother walked through the open door and past the spinning fan.

"I did what?"

"You were in a hurry. You left the dishes in the sink and then you forgot to turn off the water. A couple of dishes even floated out onto the floor when the sink overflowed. It flooded the whole apartment and Kristina's downstairs had some damage too."

"I did no such thing," Mother said.

Father shrugged. "You left after I took Celeste to school this morning. It had to be you."

"Well it wasn't."

"The door was locked and the water was on."

Mother walked into the kitchen. She stood looking around for a minute. "I remember setting the breakfast dishes up to soak," she muttered. She didn't say anything more for a long time. "But I'm sure I turned the water off."

"Do you *remember* turning off the water?" Father asked.

Mother shook her head. "I do it every day. You can't remember something like that. Did you lock your car when you got out?"

"What's that got to do with it?"

"I'll bet you think you did but you can't really remember doing it. It's the same with the water. I turn it off every day without thinking about it. I don't remember turning it off this morning but I just can't believe I would forget to do it."

Mother surveyed the damage, walking deliberately from the kitchen through the living room and into the entry. "Doesn't this look suspicious to you?" She stood at the door. "I don't think dishes will float out of the sink no matter how long the water is left on. And why are those books knocked off the shelf?"

Father ran his hand through his hair. "You have a point. Before I cleaned up, there were some muddy paw prints. I just assumed they were Celeste's but she's such a fastidious cat, it's not like her to get her feet dirty."

"Do you think it was a raccoon?"

"They're smart, and they like to wash their food. Their paws are practically human hands so they could have turned on the sink. Did you leave anything out?"

Mother surveyed the room. "The dishes were dirty. And there's always Celeste's dry food. But a raccoon wouldn't be out during the day, would it?"

"Probably not. It doesn't matter. It happened in our apartment so we're responsible."

"What do you mean?"

"There's a new kid in the manager's office. He's going to get someone out tomorrow to see if any work needs to be done to our floor or Kristina's ceiling. I think our renter's insurance covers everything for us but Kristina didn't have insurance. Hopefully she didn't lose anything due to water damage."

Mother sat down on the couch next to Father. Celeste jumped into Mother's lap. She purred as Mother absentmindedly scratched her behind the ears. Cat's purrs could help any situation.

"We should cover Kristina's losses ourselves if we can. She's been a good neighbor and I'd hate to lose her as a friend."

After that, Father left to get carry-out chicken while Mother pushed Celeste off her lap and began washing the wet towels.

* * *

During the night, Celestina kept running, running, running in her wheel. The constant rattling kept Celeste awake even though she was still very tired from the previous night's adventure. She crawled under the covers with human Celeste to muffle the noise and to combat the cold from the open doors and windows and the blowing of the fans.

The squeak of the wheel penetrated the blankets and Celeste found herself immersed in a nightmare. She was running in a giant wheel, constantly climbing the wall, only to have it constantly roll under her. Beside her, the capybara ran in its own wheel. It looked over at her with big, featureless eyes that were like black holes in its head.

The capybara's wheel began shifting closer and closer to Celeste's. The capybara smiled, its lips colored red with drool that hung from big white fangs. Frantic, Celeste ran faster and faster but got nowhere. The capybara's wheel was now so close it touched her wheel, creating a terrible screeching noise as they rubbed together.

Celeste's wheel came loose and began rolling across the ground. The capybara followed her in its wheel. They raced across an open plain. The capybara's wheel was right behind her. It bumped against her wheel. Celeste's legs felt like lead; she could hardly move, but she had to keep running. The capybara's wheel pushed her from behind and suddenly the world curved up and over them so that they ran in wheels that were themselves turning an even larger wheel.

Celeste tripped. No matter how hard she tried to control her feet, her legs were just too heavy to pick up. She stumbled again. And now the capybara's wheel was turning her wheel, pushing it up the wall of the great wheel they were both in. Finally she fell. She began rolling in her wheel like clothes in a spinning dryer.

The capybara's wheel disappeared and now the capybara was running in her wheel. Each time she fell from the top of the wheel the capybara's sharp teeth snapped at her, but the rotation carried her up out of its reach only to fall again.

Celeste meowed loudly and tried to grab at the wheel with her claws. This time, when she fell, she landed on the capybara's back. She dug her claws into soft fur that was deep and thick, just like Celestina's and not at all the way she remembered the capybara's. She meowed again and clung to the monster's back.

The capybara shook. Celeste lost her grip and began to fall.

She woke to find herself lying on the floor at the side of the bed. Human Celeste was sitting up with the sheet thrown off, rubbing bright red scratch marks that covered her leg.

"Ouch," human Celeste whined. "Why did you scratch me, Celeste? I'm not going to let you sleep under the covers any more. You are a bad cat." She pouted, her dark eyebrows knitted together.

Celeste sat up and meowed an apology. She must have clawed her human when she thought she was clawing the capybara. She felt terrible. She jumped back up on the bed and licked human Celeste's wounds. She didn't want her human to think she was a bad cat or to stop loving her.

Celeste purred when human Celeste stopped rubbing her own leg and began rubbing Celeste's back. She purred as loudly as she could to let her human know she loved her and appreciated her attention.

"I'm sorry I said that. I know you didn't mean to be a bad cat. You probably just had a nightmare." She scratched Celeste between the ears. "I bet it was about the flood in the apartment yesterday. That must have been scary for a little cat like you."

A wave of guilt coursed through Celeste starting with her stomach and ending in a prickling of her ears. But the flood was an accident and if she could explain it to her humans, she was sure they would understand.

It was far more annoying that she didn't know how to tell her owner about the horrors of the capybara. She jumped off the bed and walked over to Celestina's cage. For once the hamster was quiet, curled up and sleeping. It looked just like a hair ball that Celeste might have coughed up. "Cute" was not a word to describe such a disgusting creature. She meowed at it and scraped her claws across the plastic cage.

Human Celeste sat down on the floor next to her. She picked Celeste up and put her on her lap. "I'm sorry kitty, you can't play with Celestina. She's too small. You might hurt her, even though I know you wouldn't mean to."

Celeste swatted at the cage in frustration. She remembered how the capybara had turned into Celestina in her dream and she resented the dwarf hamster more than ever. But it consistently proved impossible to communicate ideas of any complexity with humans.

She could smell breakfast cooking so she decided to drop it. She crawled out of human Celeste's lap and made her way to the kitchen.

* * *

A knock on the door awakened Celeste from her after-breakfast nap. Father and Mother let in a gray-haired, wrinkled man wearing a bunch of tools on a belt. Celeste decided not to stick around to hear about what had been damaged.

Once outside, Celeste crossed the parking lot, traveling from one low-clearance vehicle to another. A cool breeze kicked up leaves and litter as she headed for Ruby's apartment. Thoughts of the little cat had not percolated to the top of her mind earlier but she had felt them gnawing at her all morning. How was Ruby's tail?

Celeste leaped to the top of the low wooden fence surrounding the small yard outside the sliding glass doors of Ruby's apartment. From the top she could see Tiger had beaten her there. The big orange tom was pawing at the glass, trying to get the attention of someone inside.

"Hi Tiger," Celeste said. "Have you talked to Ruby yet?"

Tiger swiveled his head and shone his yellow eyes at her. "No. She won't come to the door. I don't think her humans are home. They locked her in."

Celeste jumped down next to Tiger and peered through the glass. At first it was hard to see anything but her reflection. Then she made out a dining table and chairs and beyond them a small sofa. Moving her head back and forth to see between the obstacles inside the apartment, Celeste thought she could see Ruby lying on the back of the couch.

"Ruby!" she meowed as loudly as she could. "Ruby! It's me and Tiger. Come to the door." The form on the couch stirred. Now Celeste was certain it was Ruby. Couldn't she hear them? "Ruby, come over. Why are you locked up? Is everything okay? How's your tail?"

"Is that her back there?" Tiger asked, gesturing toward the sofa. "She looks funny. What's on her head?"

Celeste shifted position until she could see through the shadow a tree cast on the glass, letting her look inside instead of at her own reflection. She saw what Tiger was talking about. Something large and white floated around Ruby's head.

"Ruby, are you okay?" Celeste called even more loudly. She was starting to feel concerned. "What's going on? Why won't you talk to us?"

"Go away," Ruby's voice came muffled through the door. "Go away. I want to be alone."

"Something's wrong," Tiger said.

Celeste looked at him sideways. Tiger had a way of saying the obvious as if he conveyed actual news. She turned her attention back to Ruby. "What happened? You can tell us."

"We're worried about you, Ruby," Tiger added.

The cat on the couch shifted position. Celeste saw that she had a white plastic cone snapped around her neck. The cone extended past the end of her face, blocking her vision and movement in all directions.

Slowly Ruby slid down from the back of the sofa onto the cushions and then to the floor. She performed each movement carefully and deliberately, completely lacking the youthful bounce that was her hallmark.

"Look what they did to me," Ruby said when she got to the door. "And I feel funny. I think they drugged my food."

"What about the cone? Why do you have that?" Tiger asked.

"To keep me from biting my tail." Ruby flicked her tail around to where they could see it. "They took me to the vet," she murmured.

"Oh," Celeste said simultaneously with Tiger. She'd been to the vet a few times and it never proved pleasant. "What did they do to you?"

"I'm not sure." Ruby lay down on the floor as if too weak to stand. "I'm not sure but...but...oh, it's too horrible to say."

Tiger and Celeste exchanged looks.

"Is it about your tail?" Tiger asked.

Celeste almost banged her head against the glass in frustration. "It's obviously about her tail," she hissed, hoping Ruby wouldn't hear. In a louder voice she added, "Tell us what happened."

"I didn't think my tail looked that bad and neither did Sheldon—that's Audrey's older brother—but Audrey and Mother just kept going on and on about it and how terrible it was and how I had to go to the vet. So they took me to the emergency vet."

"The *emergency vet*," Celeste and Tiger repeated, their voices shaking.

"Yes. They locked me in a crate. And the emergency vet said I needed an operation but it could wait until morning. Then they left me there *overnight!*"

"Overnight!" Tiger and Celeste repeated, apparently developing a case of echolalia.

"I was so scared. When Audrey and Mother left, the vet gave me a shot. After that I couldn't think straight and I could hardly meow. There were other cats there too and I could hear them crying in the night. And dogs barking. It was horrible."

"Horrible," Celeste and Tiger said together. Celeste thought it sounded worse than her nightmare about the capybara.

"In the morning I had the operation."

Celeste was almost too afraid to ask. "What operation?"

Ruby turned her head away and hid her eyes behind the floppy white cone. "I think they cut off the end of my tail," she whispered.

"The end of your tail?" Tiger and Celeste said together.

Ruby mewed plaintively. "I can't see it because of the cone. Can you look and see if it looks any shorter?" She lifted her tail and cautiously brought it forward to where the other cats could see.

The tail was wrapped in a big white bandage that went from the tip almost to its base. The bandage made the tail look twice as thick as it really was. Celeste couldn't determine if it was shorter or not. It actually looked longer, but that was probably because of the bandage.

"It looks fine," Tiger said hopefully. "Maybe they just straightened it."

"*No limb serves a cat so well as its long, flexible, healthy tail,*" Ruby chanted mournfully.

"You know, those old cats' tales aren't really true," Celeste said. "They just sound nice. Lots of cats don't even have tails. Remember Maximilian, that big Manx cat that used to live in Building Four? His tail was two inches long at most. And he said all Manx cats are like that because they come from the Isle of Man so they don't have tails, just like men don't have tails."

"Really?" Ruby and Tiger said together.

"Tiger, don't you remember Max? Ruby might be too young, but you lived here then."

"I guess. I never really talked to him because..." Tiger turned away.

"Because why?" asked Ruby.

"I know it was stupid but I was scared of him 'cause he didn't have a tail. He didn't look like a regular cat, you know what I mean?"

"You mean he looked like a freak," Ruby said, her voice deep with emotion. "You mean I'm going to look like a freak."

"No, no, no!" Celeste said. "He did not look like a freak and you are not going to look like a freak. You're a very pretty little cat, Ruby, and even if you are missing the tip of your tail, it's not going to change that."

Ruby tried to put her head on her paws but the cone flapped around under her chin. "Let's talk about something else."

Tiger said, "Let's talk about how we're going to catch the giant hamster."

"Yeah," Ruby agreed. "That hamster is scary but I still want to catch it."

"You do? After everything that's happened, you both still want to catch the capybara?"

"Catch the capybara! Catch the capybara!" Tiger and Ruby echoed.

Celeste didn't know what to think. Her friends were both so brave. And they had so much confidence in her. Yet she did not know what to do next. She had no idea how to capture the capybara. Her first two plots had failed miserably, with Tiger injured in the first and now Ruby losing the tip of her tail.

Inside the apartment, Ruby got to her feet. She stood on her hind legs and put her front paws on the glass. "Catch the capybara!" she cried.

Tiger stood up and put his feet opposite Ruby's. "Catch the capybara!"

Celeste had no choice. She placed her paws on the glass so that the three of them were as close as possible, "Catch the capybara," she said, although with less enthusiasm than the others.

* * *

Chapter Five
How (not) to tie a noose

On her way back to the apartment, Celeste caught a whiff of a strange odor. She lifted her nose and sniffed again. It was capybara. She turned her head first left then right, trying to locate the source. Following the scent trail, she came to an unfamiliar white van. Incomprehensible human writing was scrawled across its side. Celeste had never learned to read human written symbols. There was also a picture and that she did understand. It was a capybara.

She crawled under the van and out the other side where she spotted Father talking to a man. It was the same man who had released her and her friends from the trap. The same dark eyes and glasses, the same thin-lips and a smile that barely revealed his teeth.

The man caught sight of her and held her with his eyes. "That your cat?" he asked Father.

Father turned to look at Celeste. "Yeah. Why do you ask?"

"Well, I guess all black cats pretty much look the same, but I caught one just like that last night in my trap. Along with two others, a tabby and a calico."

"Really? What were you using for bait?"

"Corn. Yup, fresh corn-on-the-cob, just like my Caplynn likes it. Funny thing to catch cats like that."

Father laughed. "I guess stranger things have happened, but it's hard to imagine. I doubt you caught Celeste, though. She's not much of an adventurer. She'd rather have someone feed her than go out hunting. In fact, I'm kind of surprised to see her this far out in the parking lot." Father knelt down and called to Celeste, "Here kitty. Here kitty-kitty-kitty."

Given the nature of the current discussion, Celeste was reluctant to go to Father. He had no idea what kind of a cat she was. Adventure was her middle name. Still, Father had deflected suspicion from her for the attempts to capture the capybara.

Father scratched her between the ears and she purred vigorously to show what a friendly cat she was, not at all the type that would spend the night trying to catch a monster.

Straightening, Father asked, "So what are you going to do now? Set the traps out again?"

"'S'pose so. Got a new idea too. I'm gonna put out some speakers and broadcast calls from Caplynn's mate. That should get her to come out. She must be lonely without Lago. But then she's pretty near her time and she might be hunkering down."

"Near her time?"

"Guess I forgot to mention Caplynn's expecting. This'll be her first litter so it's got me kind of worried. A new mother like Caplynn might not know how to take care of the pups. In the wild all the females help, even if the pups are not their own. Teaches the new mothers what to do. If Caplynn has hers before I find her, they might not make it."

Celeste had been walking in and out between Father's feet and rubbing his legs but this stopped her cold. The monster was about to produce baby monsters. If something weren't done, the whole place might be overrun with capybaras. It wouldn't be safe to be a cat anymore.

"Are they born blind and hairless like baby rats?" Father asked.

The old man laughed. "Oh no. They got their eyes open from the start and as much hair as they ever have, it being sparse on them as a breed. And they start eating grass within just a couple of days. But they won't survive without their mother's milk and warmth. And I'd say they'd be needing some protection from the cats and dogs in this area, not to mention raccoons. For such large animals, the babies are pretty small, only a couple of pounds. They wouldn't last a night without their mother's protection."

"And she's expecting soon?"

"Any day. Any day." He rubbed his chin. "I sure don't want to lose those pups. The little ones are cute as the dickens. I've already got buyers for three of 'em, though she might not have that many since it's her first litter."

"Really?" Father said. "Who's buying them?"

"Mostly people keeping them as pets but there's a private zoo down in South Texas wants one."

"Do they make good pets?"

"Oh sure," the man smiled wider so that his top teeth showed. "They're smart and clean, they love people. Only thing is you have to have some land and a good-sized pond. They get pretty big."

Father nodded.

The conversation died down after that and Celeste didn't learn anything else useful. She made her way upstairs, through the cat door and into her room to rest on the window seat and think. She closed her eyes and let the sun warm her fur.

A parable ran through her mind, *Cats' best thinking is done while lying in sun.* Celeste smiled. It reminded her of Ruby. The little cat annoyed her with all her exuberance and naive trust in old cats' tales, but she was a cute little thing and they were all kittens once.

Her fur warmed quickly, one of the perks of being a black cat, and with the warmth, ideas radiated through her mind. By the time she drifted off to sleep, she had a plan.

* * *

Right after dinner Celeste headed out the door and over to Tiger's apartment. She called from outside the building and soon he appeared on the apartment steps. She ushered him to Ruby's place without telling him anything; she didn't want to have to explain everything twice.

Together, the two cats jumped down from the rail at the top of the fence onto Ruby's patio. Looking through the glass was easier in the night when it was dark outside and light inside.

Through the glass she saw Ruby lying on the back of the sofa. Audrey sat with her and stroked her back. The human's reddish hair matched the large spot of tabby fur on Ruby's side. Celeste crouched down and Tiger followed her lead; they didn't want to get the humans involved in this.

Soon Audrey turned her attention to the television and Celeste was able to catch Ruby's eye. The spotted cat stretched and yawned, clawing the back of the couch in a convincing display of indifference. She crawled down to the seat cushion and waved her bandaged tail in front of Audrey's face until the girl dismissed her. Then she ambled to the sliding glass door, made her way into the corner and hid behind the curtain for privacy.

"Can you get out tonight?" Celeste asked.

"How are you feeling?" Tiger said at the same time.

"I don't know. I'm okay. I only ate dried cat food this afternoon. They can't put drugs in that. It's *so* hard not to eat the canned food—and today they gave me tuna—but I wanted to have a clear head for tonight. My tail hurts, though." She looked straight into Celeste's eyes. "I am not afraid of the giant hamster...I mean capybara. I want to catch it." She turned to look back at Audrey through the sheer fabric, "But they don't want me to go out because of my tail and this..." Ruby swatted at the cone around her head with a forepaw. "I've got to get this thing off."

"I have a plan," Celeste said. "But I don't know how we can get you out of there."

"They won't open the door for me."

"Humans hit the door when they want someone to open it," Tiger meowed.

"It's called *knocking*," Celeste said. "Cats can't knock. What else?"

They sat in silence for several minutes until Ruby spoke up. "Sometimes they'll open up if there's a lot of noise in the hall."

"That's it! Tiger and I can cause some serious noise. We can sing at the top of our lungs."

"Can we do *I've Got Nine Lives and I've Only Used Eight?*" Tiger asked. "That's my favorite."

Celeste didn't think it a particularly good choice since the ballad told the story of a young tom and a pretty calico who fight their humans' wills to be together but ultimately get run over by a car. Still, the occasion did call for a long, mournful song.

Ruby readied herself for a dash while Celeste and Tiger went around to the open hallway and positioned themselves directly in front of Ruby's door.

Oh, Pussywillow and Whitefoot knew,
That no matter what the others said,
Their hearts and minds and love were true,
So they went behind the garden shed
They called out to the winter moon

Upon a starry night
Called upon the goddess of
The silver light...

Celeste had forgotten how beautiful the tune and the words
were. Singing it flooded her with emotion and her voice cracked
just a little. For a moment she forgot their purpose and was
surprised when Audrey's brother, Sheldon, jerked the door open,
yelling and waving his hands.

Between Sheldon's legs came a flash of white, orange and
black, but the cone caught on Sheldon's pants leg and jerked
Ruby's head around. Sheldon reached down to grab her. Instead
he caught a writhing ball of midnight-black fur.

Celeste kept her claws sheathed but it didn't take her long to
wiggle out of Sheldon's grasp. She met with the other cats behind
the hedge that blocked a row of air-conditioning units from the
view of the apartments.

"Okay," Celeste said. "First we need to get this plastic thing
off Ruby. Lower your head so I can see how it works."

The plastic cone bent and kinked as she pressed and bit it.
She managed to make two small puncture holes with her canine
teeth but she wouldn't be able to rip it off that way. She sat back
to think.

Tiger took her place. He added two new holes to the thin
material. Then, using his big paws, he spun the cone around
Ruby's neck. "That's pretty loose," he said at last. "Let me try
pulling it off. Put your ears forward and stick your neck out as
straight as you can."

Ruby made her head and neck as thin as possible and Tiger grabbed the edge of the cone with his teeth. "Mrew?" he said unintelligibly.

Ruby dug her claws into the grass. "Go ahead."

With his large size and greater strength, Tiger completely overpowered Ruby. Her claws ripped up chunks of green grass as she lost her footing. Suddenly, the two cats were rolling all over each other. The cone crinkled and crackled but remained firmly around Ruby's neck.

"Meeeeow!" Ruby cried in pain. Tiger's hind feet crushed the bandaged section of her tail as he regained his feet. "Get off! Get off!"

Jumping to the side, Tiger nearly landed on Celeste. "Well, it *almost* worked."

"Oh, my little head. I'm lucky to still have ears." Ruby reached a paw up to brush her ear but the cone got in the way so she whimpered instead.

"It almost worked?" Celeste wondered aloud.

"I guess," Ruby said. "I mean I think so."

"We came close," Tiger added. "If we could have held on a little longer, I'm sure we would have gotten it."

An idea raced around Celeste's mind. "Let me see." She approached the younger cat and, instead of pulling or turning, attempted to put her paw between the cone and Ruby's neck. It slid in easily. Tiger was right, the cone was pretty loose. She supposed the vet wanted it to move as easily as possible while still trapping the wearer within. But there were ways around that.

"Come on." She got to her feet and headed toward the community pool. "I have an idea."

The three cats traveled as stealthily as possible. If Sheldon still looked for her, Ruby would be easy to spot with that white cone broadcasting her movements. Keeping close to the buildings and out of the glare of lights from windows, they made their way to the pool house.

"What are we going to do here?" Tiger asked.

Ruby whispered, *"Though water may pour down from the sky, a cat's fur is always dry."* Her voice trailed off. "I don't like getting wet."

"Don't worry," Celeste said. "We're not going in the pool. But we do need something to lubricate your neck so we can slip the cone off."

"The cone doesn't slip off," Tiger said.

"What does *lubricate* mean?" Ruby asked.

"Lubricate means we're going to make your neck and ears slippery. That'll let the cone come off over them even though it's pretty tight. I know they have stuff like that in here." She crouched down to crawl through a hole where one of the long vertical boards that composed the shed's walls had warped away from the others. "Tiger, wait out here with Ruby. She can't get in like that."

Celeste squeezed inside, then paused to let her eyes adjust to the darkness. She began a more-or-less systematic search. Most of the containers were closed. Celeste knocked them off the shelves, hoping they would open when they hit the concrete floor.

"Everything okay in there?" Tiger called.

"Fine," Celeste replied. "Searching is pretty noisy. Let me know if anyone is coming." Tiger didn't respond so she started knocking things down again. Finally she found what she wanted. A glass jar had broken open, spilling thick greenish goop in a blob on the floor.

Walking carefully through the shattered remains of several jars, Celeste found a small yellow cloth. She spread it out next to the broken jar of goop and pushed the still intact lid onto it. Using her paws, she dragged the cloth and the lid through the same crack where she had entered.

"Tiger, help me smear this all over Ruby's neck. And her ears. And the top and bottom of her head. But stay away from her eyes, her nose and her mouth."

Tiger sniffed the lid. "What is that stuff?"

"I don't know its real name, Father just called it goop. He used it once when Celeste got her hand stuck in a plastic tube while they were playing in the pool." She shuddered. How could her humans *play* in the water?

The two cats scooped the goop up in their paws. Ruby lowered her head. She cringed at the application of each pawful but managed to hold still. Eventually her head and neck, a large fraction of her back and most of the white cone were covered with green slime that smelled slightly like a human baby. A big dab had landed on Ruby's nose. The little cat mewed plaintively until Tiger rubbed it off with his paw.

Celeste sat back to admire their work. She'd never seen a cat look more miserable, but that wasn't the point. "That should do it. Now we need a good place to pull from."

They found an acceptable location where Ruby could brace herself against a piece of wood and the other cats would have solid footing. Celeste searched the cone for a goop-free spot and sank her teeth through the plastic on the bottom left. Tiger did the same to the top right. On Celeste's growled command, they pulled together as hard as they could while Ruby braced herself.

Celeste's teeth hurt and she had begun to consider giving up when she felt the cone slip a little. She and Tiger put in one final great effort and the cone popped off Ruby's head.

Celeste tumbled backward, dragging the cone with her since it was stuck on her teeth. The same was true for Tiger. The two cats lay in the dirt, shaking their heads, with the cone between them. Goop spattered everything, but finally they were free.

The urge to lick herself clean nearly overwhelmed Celeste but, as she had told the others before they started, the goop might be poisonous. They could rub themselves off on the grass but they'd have to get their humans' help to get really clean.

"All right," Celeste said after a good long roll. "Now it's time to go after the capybara."

"How do we do it?" Tiger asked.

Ruby mewed pitifully. "Oh Celeste, I don't know if I can stand having this goop all over me. It itches."

Rolling hadn't done much to rid the calico of her slimy covering. Instead it had thinned out and spread over more of her body. Her pretty eyes looked out from a face where the hair was slicked down and back, giving her a gaunt, wet appearance.

"On the bright side," Celeste said, "I'll bet you're not thinking about your tail much."

"You're right. I forgot all about it." Her voice sounded more normal than it had all day. "How do we catch the capybara?"

"Wait a minute." Celeste squeezed back through the loose board and into the pool shed. She jumped to a counter to avoid the mess on the floor. She leaped to a shelf that ran along the far wall where several pieces of rope hung on hooks. They were thick, yellow plastic things that humans used to tie floats in the pool. She grabbed a couple of lengths in her mouth and dragged them outside.

She told Tiger and Ruby about the owner's plan to lure the capybara with sound. "All we have to do is find the speakers and figure out which direction the capybara will come from."

* * *

They reached the tall grass around the pond and stood with their ears perked, listening. "I hear it!" they said in unison.

"It's that way." Celeste pointed with her nose.

She and Tiger each picked up a piece of rope in their mouths and the trio started off, pausing frequently to listen. The sounds of the capybara were eerie and frightening. There were clicks and squeaks, short barks and deep purrs. Celeste wondered if capybaras had a language, if any of the various and bizarre sounds they made meant anything to them or whether it was just as unintelligible to another capybara as it was to a cat. If it was a language, what sort of things did they say? And why did the capybara talk to itself all the time?

"Do you think capybaras can sing?" Ruby asked, as if reading Celeste's thoughts. "That's what it sounds like, a little, don't you think? Maybe it's a ballad like the one about Pussywillow and Whitefoot."

Celeste spat out her rope so she could speak more easily. "No. No. Capybaras are dumb, just like Celestina. They are just giant hamsters after all, and hamsters have got to be the dumbest animals ever. They spend all night running around in a wheel that doesn't go anywhere and they never even notice." The hair rose along her spine as she remembered her dream.

"Oh," Ruby said. "I was just wondering. When the capybara was trying to get us the other night, I thought...I thought..."

"What?" Celeste demanded.

"I thought it acted pretty smart. I mean, it got the corn and it didn't get caught. And it ran away before the man came. That field isn't too big so wouldn't the capybara have to be smart to keep from getting caught?"

Celeste picked up the rope again and resumed walking. She didn't want to believe the capybara was smart. It was just a giant, ugly version of Celestina and almost completely devoid of a brain.

They found the speaker tucked into tall grass in a dark section of the field near the pond but away from the road. Cattails hid it from view, presumably so the capybara wouldn't notice the sounds didn't actually come from another capybara. Obviously, the humans also thought capybaras were dumb. A cat could never be fooled by such a contrivance.

Only two paths led to the small clearing in front of the speaker. Celeste purred to herself. It was exactly the setup she'd hoped for.

Celeste dropped the rope. "This is what we're going to do. The capybara will come along one of these paths. We'll set the rope on the ground and make a noose out of it. One for each of the paths. And one of us will watch each of the ropes and give a great tug when the capybara puts its foot into the noose."

"What's a noose?" Ruby asked.

"It's a loop in the rope. If something is in the noose, the loop can't come out."

"The capybara weighs more than the three of us combined. How are we going to hold it?" Tiger asked.

Celeste purred at her own cleverness. "We're going to wrap our end around something first."

Tiger raised his whiskers, "Why would we do that?"

"It'll make us stronger."

Tiger shook his head so hard his ears flapped back and forth. "I don't get it. How can wrapping the rope around something make us stronger? That doesn't make any sense."

"I know. It doesn't make any sense to me either. But I saw human Celeste doing it for a homework assignment and it really worked. It made her as strong as Father."

"She caught a capybara with a noose?" Tiger asked.

"No. She used a rope wrapped around a table leg and was able to pull Father's hand toward her even though he didn't want her to."

"Did she use a noose?" Tiger said.

Celeste's whiskers twitched. It took so long to explain things to Tiger. "That's not the point. The noose will let us grab the capybara and wrapping the rope around something will make us strong enough to hold it."

"Will it make me strong enough?" Ruby asked.

Since they'd only found two pieces of rope and since only two trails led to the clearing, they didn't really need Ruby's help. But Celeste couldn't tell her that. "Tiger is strong enough to hold on by himself, but I can use your help."

"Okay," Ruby said. "Let's do it." She picked up one of the ropes in her mouth and headed down the path. Celeste and Tiger trotted after her.

"This looks like a good spot," Celeste said. "We can lay the noose out and push some leaves over it. Then we can hide in the bushes. Let's wrap the rope around one of those saplings."

They laid the first rope out and wrapped it all the way around the trunk of a tiny tree. That part seemed fine. The noose proved more difficult. While Celeste had seen ropes with nooses in them, mostly on TV, she'd never paid attention to the details of how they were made. They just looked like a loop in the rope. She took the end of the rope and curled it around so there was an open circle in it big enough for a capybara paw. Even though it didn't make any sense, it *looked* right.

Humans knew things cats didn't, like how to change channels on the TV by pressing buttons on a black plastic rectangle. The noose was another of those mysterious things that only humans understood. That didn't mean she couldn't use it. After all, she could step on the remote to change channels, she didn't need to understand how it worked.

She left Ruby with the first rope and went with Tiger to set up the second. Once she had him settled, rope in his mouth and hidden behind the trunk of a tree, she went back to Ruby. The two cats stood side by side, the plastic rope stretched between them. Celeste sank her teeth in as deeply as possible, trying to get a grip strong enough to hold the capybara.

And then they waited.

The clicking, squeaking and occasional bark that came out of the loudspeaker drifted over the marsh like wails of a ghost. Celeste huddled next to Ruby, glad for the little cat's company and forgetting for a moment how filthy and slimy she was. Neither cat made a sound, nor could they hear Tiger, though he wasn't far away.

After what seemed like hours, Celeste heard musical clicking coming from the darkness in the opposite direction from the loudspeaker. Ruby must have heard it too because Celeste could feel her muscles tense. They crouched lower, hiding as best they could in the twigs and branches of the brush.

The clucks and squeals got louder. Celeste looked down the path. She couldn't see anything; the moon had not risen yet and the night was dark.

"Click, click, click, click, click." The rapid series of noises sounded like a woodpecker playing the flute. A deep, almost inaudible thrumming caused the hair on her back to stand up. Celeste did not fancy herself a scaredy-cat but there were times when any cat got scared, and this was one of them.

The capybara emerged from the void as a creeping darkness. Its wide body filled the trail, brushing against the weeds and shrubs on either side as it waddled forward. It held its head low, so that its nose was no higher than its knees and the great hunched bulk of its body followed after, swaying with each ponderous step.

Celeste wanted to flee but she forced herself to remain still. Just a few more feet and the monster would step into the noose. Then they would tug the rope, closing the loop around its deformed foot and call for Tiger's help. With the setup they were using, three cats could easily bring down even the largest capybara. They were predators after all, and the capybara was a prey animal. Still, she wished it had chosen Tiger's path.

The capybara paused. It raised its nose and sniffed the air. If it had any intelligence it would surely notice that even if the speakers put out capybara sound, they did not emit capybara scent.

For a long time it stood, testing the air and flicking its little ears. Celeste watched as it lifted one front paw in preparation for a step but too uncertain to take it. The foot was black and almost completely bald. Three large toes sported thick, blunt claws. They curled together with a much smaller toe way up on the outside of the foot. The small toe looked almost like a human thumb except Celeste was pretty sure thumbs were on the inside of the hand not the outside. The feet looked powerful. She needed to avoid them if it came to a fight.

The speaker emitted a plaintive squeak and the capybara squeaked back, then stepped forward. One more step and its foot landed smack-dab in the middle of the noose.

As one, Celeste and Ruby pulled with all their weight on the rope. It went tight in their mouths, pulling plastic against teeth and gums. Celeste called to Tiger through clenched teeth.

They had the capybara!

The animal turned its dark eyes toward them but didn't move. Celeste growled and hissed through a mouthful of rope.

The capybara seemed not to understand. It stood in the trail, swinging its blunt head back and forth as if trying to comprehend what was happening.

Leaping out of the weeds, Tiger landed squarely on the capybara's back. It let out a horrible screech as Tiger sank his claws in. Then the capybara moved, demonstrating surprising agility for an animal that the instant before had the mobility of a boulder.

Celeste caught just the impression of the capybara spinning like a top when she found herself bowled over backward on top of Ruby. The noose had not held. Since the cats had wrapped the rope around the tree trunk, their backward spill took them directly into the path of the whirling capybara. Celeste grabbed with both front paws and managed to attach herself to the rear of the animal. Meanwhile one of the capybara's huge feet landed squarely on Ruby's bandaged tail. The little calico screamed like she was dying.

Ruby's scream must have scared the capybara even more. It reversed its spin in a sudden movement that caught both of its passengers by surprise. Celeste flew off, landing heavily on Ruby, who screamed again. Tiger managed to stay on for another full rotation, then he, too, was violently ejected, landing on Celeste and knocking her back onto Ruby. Only a deep "whoosh" as the air was knocked out of her escaped from Ruby's lungs.

Free of its attackers, the capybara ran full speed back down the trail. Tiger regained his feet and chased after it with Celeste close behind.

The capybara did a good impression of a racehorse as it dashed along the dark, narrow trail. Celeste couldn't see anything ahead of her except Tiger's tail and hind legs but she could hear the heavy footfalls of the galloping capybara.

The drumbeat of the capybara's progress changed but Celeste realized too late what it meant. She crashed into Tiger, who had set his heels into the soft soil in an attempt to stop. The two of them tumbled into the water.

Celeste gasped when she finally got her head above the surface. Her feet flailed in every direction, connecting only with Tiger and not with the bottom. She tried to climb on top of Tiger's head but he sank underneath her. She had to release her claw-grip on him to keep from sinking herself. As Tiger slipped below her last toe, she found herself swimming for the first time in her life. She did not like it.

Celeste struggled to shore. Tiger splashed behind her, only the slightest whimper escaping from his lips. And down the path came the bedraggled and limping form of Ruby, covered with goop and mud. The bandage on her tail looked as if it had never been white. She plopped down in the mud next to Celeste and Tiger.

The cats lay panting in the muddy trail, too tired to move or talk.

Finally Tiger coughed. "We almost had it."

Celeste glared at him. Tiger smiled a little, his face covered in dark red wounds inflicted by Celeste's claws.

"Yeah," Ruby's voice was hardly above a whisper. "Almost." She gulped a few breaths of air. *"A cat that still has all nine lives, hasn't lived because he hasn't died,"* Ruby quoted the saying mother cats used to encourage timid kittens.

Celeste mustered enough strength to put her paws over her ears.

* * *

Chapter Six
How (not) to be brave

Celeste startled awake. She jumped to her feet and spun around. Her feet slipped out from under her in the mud. She fell, landing on Ruby.

Ruby squealed. "What happened? Where are we?"

"Quiet," Celeste whispered. "I think something's coming." With one of her back paws she nudged Tiger, who lay lifelessly in the center of the trail. He hardly stirred, so Celeste nudged him again.

"I'm sore," Tiger said, still half-asleep. "Leave me alone or I'll claw you."

"Get up," Celeste urged him. "I heard something."

Tiger sprang to his feet, every hint of exhaustion vanished. "Was it the capybara?"

"I don't know. Something woke me. I didn't hear it well." She turned her head from side to side, trying to locate the sound again. There was nothing except the chirping of frogs and the constant hum of traffic on the highway.

"I don't hear anything," Tiger's voice broke the quiet.

"Me either," Ruby said.

"That's it!" Celeste said, finally realizing what had eluded her. "I don't hear a capybara."

"It probably ran away after I chased it into the water," Tiger said.

Celeste hissed in frustration. "No, I don't hear the capybara on the speaker. Listen."

They sat in silence for a moment.

"The capybara's owner must have turned the recording off." Celeste said. "We can't let him find us."

"I don't want to go to the pound," Ruby whimpered.

Celeste looked around. "We have the advantage; humans can hardly see in the dark. Follow me." She started down a trail that skirted the edge of the pond.

The moon had come up and risen to near zenith. That meant it was after midnight but not yet close to dawn. Celeste had not expected the man to come to check on the trap during the night. She wondered if he did that because of their previous incident. Was he looking for cats? Why couldn't she hear him? He had to be close by if he turned off the speaker.

With Ruby directly behind her and Tiger picking up the rear, Celeste made her way down the path, almost as if she were stalking prey. She raised each paw, listened, then placed it gently back on the ground only inches in front of its previous position. By their silence, she knew Tiger and Ruby were doing the same.

She'd never seen a pound. She'd been born into a loving household of humans who had been friends of Mother and Father. Once adopted, she'd become an integral part of the family. Her humans would never take her to the pound. And she'd never strayed or gotten lost. She knew she was living the good life for a cat. Even so, she sometimes wondered what a more exotic existence might be like. She'd heard that barn cats climbed into hay lofts, caught mice, attacked and killed fierce rats, and drank milk every day fresh from a cow. It sounded a lot more exciting than her life. But then she'd also heard that barn cats who didn't catch their quota of rodents could suffer a worse fate than the pound. She wondered if it was true that—

Foot in mid-air, Celeste froze. Had there been a sound? She shouldn't have let her mind drift. Maybe she imagined it. It had been almost too low even for a cat's sensitive hearing. She waited, listening.

"Why are we stopping?" Ruby whispered.

"Sssh." For a long moment there was nothing. Finally, Celeste put her foot down and lifted the next. No sound. She took another step.

She froze. Had she heard one of the capybara's clicks? After what felt like hours, she began moving again. The capybara was prey. It was not as if she needed to worry about it stalking them.

Still, she didn't want to come upon it unexpectedly. She'd had enough capybara for one night.

Only a few steps later she stopped again. Was there a frog whose chirp sounded like the capybara? Maybe that was what she kept hearing. The sound, faint and indistinct as it was, made the hair on her back stand on end. She had gone down this path a million times before; she couldn't believe it could be as scary as it seemed now.

She turned to get a sight of her friends, needing the reassurance of their trusting faces.

"Is everything okay, Celeste?" Ruby asked.

Celeste didn't answer. Beyond Ruby, and beyond Tiger's bulky outline, stood a dark, hulking shadow. Celeste couldn't speak.

"Celeste?" Tiger said from what should have been the back of the line. "What's wrong?"

Celeste's throat produced a low "Mrreow." She couldn't form words. Moonlight glinted off the shadow's dank, dark eyes. Now there could be no doubt. The monster had followed them. It had walked in their tracks. It–

"Click, click, click." The capybara spoke at full volume and the noise thundered through the tense silence.

Tiger shot straight up into the air, back arched, fangs bared, claws at the ready.

Ruby spun around, but her injuries made her slow and stiff. She couldn't turn in place. When she saw the capybara, her eyes went so wide Celeste thought they might pop out of her face.

Tiger came down, landing squarely on Ruby's back. The little cat went down under his weight, hardly struggling.

"Click, click, click, click, squeak, click," the capybara said.

Panicked, Celeste tore off down the path. She could hear Ruby and Tiger behind her but she didn't slow down to look back. Before, they might have nearly caught the capybara, but now the capybara had almost caught them.

Reaching the metal fence, Celeste pushed through without breaking pace. The pavement felt good under her feet–hard, substantial, familiar. She skidded under a car and kept going. Finally she stopped under Father's car in her own parking lot. Tiger slid in beside her and the two cats sat panting, unable to speak.

When she finnally caught her breath, Celeste turned to Tiger. "Where's Ruby?"

Tiger looked around. "She's not here."

"I *know*. What happened to her?"

"I don't know. I landed on her and she fell down. The capybara was right there. I could see its teeth. It has *enormous* teeth." Tiger paused. "You don't think..."

Celeste felt hollow inside. How could they have run away and left their friend behind? It made them no better than dogs. The creature was a monster. If anything happened to Ruby, Celeste could only blame herself. She had decided to track down and capture the "giant hamster." And she'd kept at it even after she had seen its tremendous proportions, and how little it resembled a hamster.

For a time, neither cat spoke. Celeste was glad for the silence. If only she could make peace with her thoughts. She kept imagining poor little Ruby, her tail already broken and bandaged, her body covered with green slime, badly bruised by many direct hits from flying cats, now just lying there, waiting for the capybara to finish her off.

"She was a good cat," Tiger said at last.

Celeste nodded, her throat too tight to speak.

"We have to go back for her. We have to know what happened."

"Curiosity killed the cat," Celeste said flatly. She knew Tiger was right, but she did not know if she could force herself do it. She had never been so scared in her life. She didn't think she could face that fear again.

"Please say you'll come, Celeste," Tiger's voice was uncharacteristically high-pitched. "I know it's my fault. I shouldn't have landed on her. And I shouldn't have run off without her. I'm the big cat. I'm supposed to be strong and brave. I don't know what happened to me. But I can't go back alone." His eyes pleaded. "I'm too scared." He put his head on his paws.

It hurt Celeste to see Tiger blaming himself, but it made her feel braver too. "No, Tiger. It's my fault. Chasing the giant hamster was my idea. None of this would have happened if it weren't for me." After a pause she continued, "What's important now is that Ruby needs our help."

Celeste crawled out from under Father's car and waited for Tiger to join her. Once she had his large frame by her side, she felt a thousand times better.

"Can you whistle?" Tiger asked.

Celeste shook her ears, not sure she'd heard right. "What?"

"Can you whistle?"

"Of course I can't whistle. No cat can. Only humans whistle."

"That's too bad. My owner sings a song sometimes about whistling. The song says that if you whistle, then you're not afraid."

It occurred to Celeste that Tiger might never have been afraid before tonight. "We don't need to whistle, Tiger. We have something humans don't have. We have nine lives."

"Do you think that's true?"

"I don't know. Maybe. Cats are pretty lucky animals."

"Yeah," Tiger said, "Except for Ruby."

Tiger's tone made the bottom fall out of Celeste's stomach. She struggled to keep a brave front. "We don't know that. Ruby could be fine. Maybe she caught the capybara by herself and is waiting for us to come back. She'll be standing on its back, meowing to the world."

"Ruby couldn't catch a mouse. You're making a joke."

"She's full of surprises. Isn't there a saying, *The littlest cat catches the biggest rat?*"

"If there is, Ruby knows it."

They headed off, their spirits slightly raised, thinking about how Ruby might even now be feasting on capybara meat. It wasn't until they reached the turn onto the path by the pond that they became somber again. They didn't speak and Celeste was glad not to have to share her dismal thoughts.

The falling moon cast long shadows across the dark trail. Celeste walked side-by-side with Tiger, not wanting to risk losing the big cat. She remembered watching a TV show with Mother and Father one night where each member of a group of brave but scared friends was picked off one-by-one by a psychopathic killer. She shivered and moved closer to Tiger.

"You're pushing me off the trail, Celeste. Move over."

Embarrassed, Celeste forced herself to walk more toward her side of the path.

They had almost reached the point where they last encountered the capybara. Celeste could see her pawprints and Tiger's larger ones in the soft mud. There were no prints from any other animals. Whatever happened after they left, neither Ruby nor the capybara had come this way.

Celeste slowed as they neared the final bend. She wanted Tiger to go first. But Tiger slowed to match her pace until they were both standing still. No sound reached them from either cat or capybara and the only scents were of marsh grass and mud.

"What do we do now?" Tiger asked in a whisper.

Although her voice cracked with fear, Celeste managed to call out, "Ruby? Ruby? Are you there?"

No answer.

She wasn't sure it meant anything. Her voice had boomed in her ears but she knew that it had not really been that loud. She called again, this time managing a normal speaking volume.

No answer.

Celeste took a step forward. Her heart warmed and her courage increased when Tiger shadowed her.

"We're in this together," he said.

The irony was not lost on Celeste. Although Tiger certainly believed his words, they had both abandoned Ruby. She steeled herself and vowed never to do such a thing again. But at least a part of her wondered if she could keep that promise.

A few more steps and they were around the bend.

"They're not here," Tiger said. "Either one of them."

Celeste could see that. The grass had been trampled into the mud, cat and capybara footprints abounded, and bits of white, black and orange fur could be found clinging to the ends of sharp branches. "That's a good sign," she said. "The capybara couldn't have moved Ruby. She must be alive and able to walk."

"Where is she?"

"Ruby! Ruby!" Celeste called, this time using the full strength of her voice. "Ruby, where are you? Come out." But only the frogs called back.

Looking at the tracks and scattered fur, Celeste realized she'd learned a lot from TV. For instance, she knew how to examine a crime scene. She told Tiger to stand to one side and began systematically examining the evidence. The bits of cat hair told her very little. She was black, Tiger was orange and Ruby was black and white and orange. So the fur could belong to all three cats or it could all be Ruby's. No information there.

Next she examined the footprints. The pawprints of the capybara were enormous next to Ruby's tiny ones. Its blunt claws dug deeply into the mud where Ruby's hardly dented the surface. From this, Celeste verified her own experience that the capybara weighed significantly more than the cat.

"Look here," Tiger pointed his nose at some broken branches at one edge of the clearing.

"In a minute. I'm still working on my investigation."

In the center of the clearing, the paw tracks went every-which-way. Some of the cat prints were larger than others and Celeste reasoned that these must be Tiger's. She circled around, trying to follow the action indicated by the prints, but found it impossible. As she got closer to the edge, she encountered fewer prints, especially toward the direction of the loudspeaker.

Methodically, she made her way around and around until she came to where Tiger stood. Here both the cat and the capybara prints all pointed in one direction.

"Look," Tiger said. "I think they went this way."

Celeste examined the broken branches along with the footprints. She pushed past Tiger and took a couple of steps into the brush. "I think you're right. They broke through here. Look at this print. See how Ruby's print is inside the capybara's? She was following it."

"So Ruby's all right!"

Celeste shook her head, "I don't know. This is Ruby's right front paw. See how the print isn't as deep as the others? She's not putting all her weight on this foot. She must be hurt."

"But she's still chasing the giant hamster."

"Maybe." Celeste hadn't done much investigative work before, but it looked to her as if both the cat and the capybara had left these footprints at a walk. "I think we should follow them."

"Oh," Tiger's voice squeaked with apprehension. He crouched low to the ground and looked down the trail. "It's so dark."

By now the moon hung low in the western sky and Celeste could see a hint of blue to the east. She didn't like waiting but the thought of traveling down that dark trail in pursuit of a monster sent a shiver all the way to the tip of her tail. The trail lay in deep shadow and they might miss the tracks in the dark. "We can wait until dawn. It can't be more than a half-hour."

Tiger sighed with relief.

Celeste curled herself up in a ball in the driest part of the clearing and Tiger lay down next to her so that their backs touched. "Ruby isn't dead," she said to assure both Tiger and herself. "Things will look better in the daylight."

"Once it's light we'll find Ruby and if she hasn't done it for us already, we'll catch that capybara," Tiger whispered. His voice was thick with exhaustion. Soon Celeste could feel his breathing become deep and regular as he slid into sleep.

Celeste didn't fall asleep easily. She couldn't keep herself from thinking about the pawprints and what they meant. Ruby had limped off in the same direction as the capybara. She'd been following it. Celeste was no expert on capybaras, but its prints looked even and regular. She suspected the creature was in perfect health despite its several skirmishes with cats over the last few days. It made no sense for an injured Ruby to pursue it on her own. But what else could the tracks mean?

* * *

With the dawn, a thick fog rose from the marsh, swallowing the muddy shore with its brambles and saplings and waking

Celeste when a cold drop of water collected on a leaf and spilled into her ear.

Rising with a yawn and a stretch that resulted in a nice set of claw marks in the mud in front of her, Celeste greeted the day with a mixture of dread and enthusiasm. She poked Tiger. "Time to get up. We need to find Ruby."

Tiger rolled onto his back, rubbing his head against the ground and folding his forepaws to his chest. "Are you sure?" His eyes were tightly closed. "Can't we wait until it warms up?"

"Ruby could be in danger. We have to find her now."

He sat up and began licking himself.

"We don't have time for that," Celeste said. She longed for a good washing herself. She had never been so dirty. Her skin itched with it. Mud, sweat, green goop. Thinking about it only made it worse. "Come on, Tiger. Let's get Ruby and be home in time for breakfast."

The idea of food got Tiger moving.

Until she'd mentioned it, Celeste hadn't realized how hungry she was. After some thought she realized she'd eaten dinner last night. She hadn't actually missed any meals. Still, breakfast time approached and her stomach growled in anticipation.

The path Ruby took with the capybara didn't look as frightening in the daylight, even with fog steaming from the earth. Celeste examined the pawprints again with the benefit of light and reached the same conclusion. The trail was easy to follow; the capybara had broken numerous branches and twigs as it worked its way through the brush. Its distinctive feet left deep prints—some three-toed and some four-toed—in the soft soil.

Pushing grass out of the way with her nose, Celeste started down the trail with Tiger close behind. They progressed slowly as Celeste constantly checked the prints to make sure they didn't change direction and that Ruby and the capybara remained on the same track.

After several minutes, Celeste paused to listen.

"I heard it too," Tiger said.

"It's not far. Be extra quiet."

"Is Ruby with it?"

"I don't know but their tracks are still together."

The chirping, clicking and occasional alien purring rose in volume as they advanced. There were also small noises that could easily be ignored or missed in the hum of traffic and the calls of birds. Celeste paused, pricking her ears forward.

"Doesn't that sound like more than one?" Tiger asked.

Celeste shuddered. It took all her will to take the next step, and then the next. With each advance she thought she could go no farther.

By the time Celeste had taken ten steps, with Tiger just behind her, there could be no doubt about what they would find. The small noises must come from the small snouts of baby capybaras. And it sounded like a lot of them. Their clicks and squeaks were odd. Too similar to their mother's; not high-pitched and abbreviated the way the calls of kittens are.

Through the brush, Celeste saw the reddish hair of the capybara. The capybara sounds were constant but she didn't hear anything that sounded like a cat. She could see Ruby's pawprints still mixed with the capybara's just in front of her own feet. Ruby had to be up there.

"Should we rush them?" Tiger whispered, coming up beside Celeste.

"No, we need to see what's going on. Ruby's already hurt. We don't want to injure her any more."

Celeste pushed her nose through the tangle of leaves and branches. Finally, she could see into the clearing. Her jaw dropped open and a hiss of surprise escaped her lips.

"What is it?"

Celeste couldn't bring herself to answer.

"What do you see?" Tiger nosed up next to her. He pushed her out of the way with his shoulder.

Celeste was too stunned to protest. She couldn't take her eyes off the scene. No amount of staring could make sense of it.

The capybara lay on its side, its huge hind paws stretched out behind it and its chin resting on its forelegs. Around it ran numerous—too many for Celeste to count—baby capybaras. Each of the babies looked like a miniature of the adult, except that they had very large heads for their size. They fell down frequently, tripping over the smallest twig or pebble or—and this is what kept Celeste immobile—Ruby.

Ruby lay almost within the semi-circle formed by the capybara's body and outstretched limbs. The smallest of the infant capybaras snuggled against her side, sleeping.

* * *

Chapter Seven
How (not) to be a cat

Celeste stood with Tiger by her side, unmoving, for a long while. Her brain ceased to function, as if all it could hold was a single thought that ran through it over and over and over again: *What could make Ruby befriend the capybara?*

Eventually Tiger spoke, breaking the spell. "Do you think she's dead?"

"No." Celeste said in a harsh whisper. "She's not dead. She's breathing. Look, her tail is twitching. She's asleep." In fact, the bandage had come off Ruby's tail sometime during her ordeal. Celeste gasped when she realized the younger cat's fears had proved true. Poor Ruby! Maybe it would look better when it healed.

Tiger's voice brought her back. "But what about all those capybaras? Even Ruby could catch the baby ones. They can hardly stand."

What about the capybaras? There had to be some missing element, some key fact that Celeste did not know that would explain everything. But as long as she stared, watching every movement of the adult capybara and trying to count the babies, Celeste could think of no reason in the universe why a cat would sleep in their midst. Only one cat knew the answer to that riddle.

"Ruby!" Celeste called quietly, hoping the cat's sensitive hearing would pick up her voice without alerting the mother capybara.

When Ruby didn't move, Celeste called again, slightly louder.

"She's sleeping pretty soundly," Tiger said.

"Hurt cats need their sleep." Celeste backed out of the brush until she stood in the trail the capybara had made during the night. "We're going to have to go in. But we need a better approach. If we enter through all this vegetation, we'll be trapped."

Tiger nodded but didn't say or do anything useful.

"Let's circle around and see if there's another entrance."

Everywhere, except where the capybara's thick body had broken through, brambles with sharp spines poked the cats when they attempted to pass.

"So this is it," Tiger said when they had come full-circle. "We have to go in here, just where the capybara would expect us."

Celeste meowed in agreement, her tail twitching with displeasure at the prospect.

"I can go first. I'm bigger and stronger. And I've attacked that capybara three times now. Maybe it's a little afraid of me. Just tell me what to do, Celeste."

Tiger's bravery made Celeste feel ashamed. She had been about to ask him to go first for just the reasons he gave—plus another she didn't want to admit. She was afraid. And now that fear wasn't just that the capybara might hurt her physically. Maybe the capybara had mesmerized Ruby. Maybe if a cat looked into the dark pits of its eyes, the capybara would suck out its soul. She wanted to warn Tiger not to look in its eyes but knew it would sound ridiculous. Even Tiger, dumb as he was, wouldn't believe in thought control. So all she did was nod and, when Tiger bravely advanced, she followed.

The big cat had to crouch and wiggle his way for the last two feet. The wiry vegetation sprung back where it had not been broken. Celeste crawled behind him, worried about their retreat if they should need one.

At last, Tiger pulled himself out of the brush and stood in the clearing. Celeste quickly followed. She emerged ready for battle, but found the scene eerily quiet. Tiger stood still as a marble statue. Celeste took in the scene but avoided meeting the capybara's eyes. She discovered Ruby standing to one side of the monster with the runt baby monster huddled beneath her belly. All of the other babies had gathered behind their mother, their big eyes in their oversized heads looking like so many holes in the universe.

The mother capybara constantly whispered clicks and squeaks. With Ruby at its side, the creature's enormous stature became even more apparent. It was maybe half-again as tall as a cat but its thick body appeared about three times as wide and twice as long. The stubby legs made up little of its height. While the head did not overwhelm the adult's proportions the way the babies' heads did, it did dwarf Ruby's. And yet its mouth was tiny.

"Ruby, are you all right?" Tiger voice was hushed as if to preserve the paralysis of the scene.

"The capybaras aren't evil," Ruby replied. "They just look that way. Really, they're nice."

"What happened to you?" Celeste asked. "Do you know who you are? And what you are?"

"I'm Ruby, the cat."

"Then what are you doing?"

"*Whenever you meet with someone new,*" Ruby said in that sing-song voice she reserved for cat lore, "*this is the thing that you should do. Treat them as if you've met a friend, and it will be true by the day's end.*"

"That's ridiculous," Celeste hissed. "Did you ever try that with a dog?"

"Well, it doesn't work all the time," Ruby admitted. "But you never know unless you try. And we didn't try with the capybara."

No one spoke for a minute, except the capybara and her offspring, who kept up an incessant chatter.

"What happened?" Tiger asked.

"I don't know exactly. I blacked out after I saw the capybara behind me, I don't know why."

Tiger hung his head. "That's my fault. I jumped and landed on you. I'm really sorry."

"It's okay. When I woke up the capybara was licking my face. I was scared to death but I was hurt and couldn't get away so I stayed very still. *If you can't escape from an angry dog, try to pretend you're just a log.* I didn't have much choice, given my condition.

"The capybara licked me all over my body, especially where I was hurt. After a while I started feeling better and I could sit up. Caplynn Rous sat next to me, making that cute little chirping noise–"

"Cute? Cute! That animal is dangerous, it's not cute," Celeste broke in.

"Well, it made me feel better. When she got up and started walking through the brush, I didn't want to be left alone, so I followed her. It was hard going, even though Caplynn is built like a bulldozer. This brush has spines and stickers and they were poking us. But she always seemed to pick the thickest part."

Ruby paused when the baby capybara squeaked and poked its nose at her side. "He's hungry. He doesn't get as much as the others because he's so small, kind of like me. I was the runt of my litter."

"He's *not* like you," Celeste's voice was sharp and loud. "He's–it's–a capybara and you are a cat."

"Then what happened?" Tiger asked.

Ruby nuzzled the runt capybara. "Caplynn lay down and started having all these babies. There are eight of them. They all look pretty much alike except Rubio here is the smallest."

"Rubio? Rubio?" Celeste could not believe her ears. Did Ruby intend to name one of these abominations after herself?

Ruby self-consciously licked her paw and started cleaning her ears while she continued the story. "Rubio was born last and he's always the last to feed. And there isn't enough room next to his mom when they're all sleeping so he came to sleep next to me." She stopped cleaning her ears and looked at her two friends, not even flinching from Celeste's most severe gaze. "I'm worried about him. I think we need to find the owner and make sure he takes care of Rubio."

Celeste took a step forward. She didn't like the giant mother capybara being so close, but she imagined that a cat's speed and dexterity, along with the capybara's inherent slowness would be enough. She needed to keep Ruby talking, "Did you name any of the others?"

"Actually I did." Ruby stepped back and began nosing through the babies. She pushed one forward and it toppled and fell on its big head. "This one is Celester, after Celeste. See, he has this cute little tuff of hair on his head. And this one," she licked the biggest of the litter, "this one is Tiger Too."

Celeste seethed. She already shared her name with a human and a hamster. She would not share it with a capybara. Celester! Ugh. She had to put a stop to this. Just one more step and she could grab the baby closest to Ruby. She shifted her weight forward and picked up her paw, nice and slow.

"Bark! Bark, bark!" The adult capybara advanced.

Celeste scuttled back. The capybara seemed to know she intended to grab one of its babies. It had to be just instinct and not evidence of real intelligence. Of course the mother capybara would protect its young.

One of the babies stumbled toward her. In a way, they were kind of cute, once you got past their enormous snouts and if you didn't look at their eyes. The little creature clicked at her and shook its head playfully. This caused it to fall on its nose. It quickly regained its feet but now faced the wrong way. It looked around, obviously confused.

"I think Celester likes you," Ruby said.

The name made Celeste cringe. "I don't want one of these monsters named after me. Stop calling it that."

"I don't know," Ruby replied. "I think I did a good job. You and Celester make a good pair and look how well Tiger is getting along with Tiger Too."

While engaged in her scheme to capture one of the babies, Celeste had ignored Tiger. Now she found he had wandered to the side of the clearing where he played with one of the babies. Sitting on the ground, Tiger waited for the baby to come up to him. The little creature raised one paw and waved it at him a few times. Tiger waved a paw back. After a few waves, the baby lost its balance and fell over. Tiger waited patiently for it to regain its feet and then the game started over again.

"What are you doing?" Celeste hissed at him.

Without taking his attention from his playmate, Tiger replied, "The little ones are pretty cute. I think Tiger Too likes me."

"You can play with your food as long as you like, as long as the play ends with a bite," Celeste said. "Isn't that right Ruby? Isn't that one of the sayings your mother taught you? These things are *prey*. We are *predators*."

"I don't know, Celeste," Tiger replied. "They aren't much like mice or birds. I looked in the cage in your human's room but I didn't get a good look at the hamster. But from the way you've described them, capybaras don't seem much like them either. Look how sweet Tiger Too is!"

With disgust, Celeste noted that the baby had tired of play and now lay sleeping at Tiger's feet.

The adult capybara's squeaks became more rapid and higher pitched. The little capybaras scrambled and jostled to get closer to her, including Celester and Tiger Too. Rubio remained huddled under Ruby.

"Eep, eep, eep," the mother bleated. She began poking her nose into the brambles ringing the clearing. "Eeeep, eep, eep," the babies cried in return.

The small clearing couldn't hold that much action. Celeste found herself scurrying from one side to the other in order to avoid the lumbering monster. The babies circled like a swarm of bees at a hive. They stayed close to their mother's head and shoulders and Celeste could find no opportunity to grab one.

At last the adult capybara simply plunged into the brush. Ruby's description of her as a bulldozer gained sudden credibility. To Celeste's surprise, the babies maintained their relative position, traveling mostly underneath their mother as she plowed through the foliage rather than falling behind where Celeste could snag one.

Rubio remained snuggled between Ruby's legs. The calico swung her head back and forth between Celeste and Tiger and the disappearing form of the mother capybara. "I have to go," she said at last. She scuttled down the incipient trail just as soon as room appeared behind the mother.

"Where are you going?" Celeste called to Ruby.

"I don't know. I can't take Rubio away from his mom. At least not until we find their owner. I think something is upsetting Caplynn. She's acting really nervous."

Celeste spun around to face the original trail into the clearing. The hairs on her back raised and she felt her whiskers stick out from her face like spines. Something was coming down the path. And it had them trapped. At least until the mother capybara tunneled its way to freedom.

"What is it?" Tiger asked.

Finding the big cat at her side boosted Celeste's confidence. "I don't know. Maybe it's just a squirrel."

Tiger listened for a moment. "Bigger than a squirrel from the sound of it."

Celeste knew that. "There's no way out. We'd better pounce as soon as it reaches the clearing."

Nodding, Tiger assumed pouncing posture. His body lay flat against the soil with his legs bunched under him and the kinked end of his tail flicked like a yellow flame.

With her heart beating in her chest, Celeste crouched next to Tiger. The level of noise the animal made as it pushed its way down the narrow path indicated something a little larger than Tiger. It could be a small dog.

Nothing along the rim of the clearing was sturdy enough for them to climb. If a dog came out of that hole, they would have to fight it. Celeste exchanged glances with Tiger. "Some of those little dogs have big, bug eyes. Claw them if you get a chance."

Tiger nodded. "I can handle it, Celeste. You make a break for it as soon as you can. Go down the tunnel. I'll take care of the dog."

They had faced a lot of dangers together the last few days. And Celeste remembered the guilt she felt at abandoning Ruby, even though it had been accidental. She could face a dog more easily than her own guilt. "No, we'll do this together, Tiger. You go for the head. I'll pounce on its back."

They waited in silence. Celeste felt her ears burn with tension as she listened to the creature's approach. She detected movement through the undergrowth, a deep yellow form slinking down the trail.

"Who's there?" Celeste called.

No answer.

Through the brush, the form resolved into the outline of a cat. Celeste signed with relief. Her fears had escalated all the way up to raccoon. But a cat was one of her own kind. She meowed a friendly greeting.

As he rose to his feet after crawling through the tunnel-like entrance to the clearing, Celeste recognized Pumpkin. Behind him came two of his minions, tough toms from the fence-sitting gang. The white one with half his ear missing and bright blue eyes was Snowball. The other was Phukat.

"Well, look what we have here," Pumpkin said, his amber eyes taking in the scene. "Hello Celeste. Tiger." He nodded to the two cats.

"Hello Pumpkin," Celeste said as casually as she could.

"Nice little place you have here. Smells kind-of funny though. You smell that, Snowball?"

"Ye- yeah, Boss," the white cat's hearing wasn't good and he stuttered when he spoke.

"What do you think it is?"

"Kind-of familiar. Ha- ha- ha- hamster maybe."

The exchange sounded scripted. Snowball hadn't even bothered to pretend to sniff the air.

"Hamster, you say?" Pumpkin's voice sounded playful in the same way a cat plays with a mouse. "Do you think that's a dwarf hamster or a regular-sized hamster?"

"It don't sme- sme- smell like neither." Snowball's whiskers twitched with an inside joke. "I'd say it smells like *giant* hamster."

"Really?" Pumpkin never took his eyes off Celeste. "That's odd because just a couple of days ago Celeste here told me she was hunting after some hamster. She didn't mention it was a *giant* hamster."

Both Snowball and Phukat laughed.

"That is funny, Boss," Phukat said. "Because it's not exactly *lying* but it's not the truth either."

"Yeah," Pumpkin continued. "A clever cat like Celeste should know better than to lie."

The tip of Celeste's tail twitched uncontrollably. "I meant to tell you," Celeste lied, still not knowing any better. "But you laughed at me and I got embarrassed. I didn't think you'd care about any hamster, even a giant one."

Pumpkin casually swiped his paw across his face to clean off some mud from the trail. "Good answer, Celeste. But not good enough. Still, I'm a nice cat. I'll give you one more chance. Explain what you're doing here."

The truth didn't seem like a good idea but Celeste's mind was blank. She stood staring at the three thugs, unable to come up with anything like a reasonable excuse.

"The giant hamster got Ruby!"

Celeste swung her head to look at Tiger. Was he out of his mind?

"It got her. It uses mind control or something. She's like a zombie cat. She'll do anything it says." Tiger's words rushed out of his mouth. "I think it can hypnotize cats with its eyes."

Flicking his whiskers, Pumpkin almost laughed. "Really? That's the best you can do?"

A plan began to form in Celeste's brain. She didn't have time to think through the details but maybe Tiger's story could work for them. "He's telling the truth. The giant hamster made Ruby go with it." She half-turned. "They went down there." She indicated the new trail made by the mother capybara. "We wanted to help her but we were scared."

"Check it out," Pumpkin ordered Snowball. He turned his attention back to Celeste and Tiger. "Explain some more."

"We were looking for Ruby all night," Celeste said. "We finally found her in this clearing. I think it was just a few minutes before you arrived, but I can't be sure. She was guarding the giant hamster. When we tried to talk to her, she wouldn't listen. She kept saying the monster was cute...and she named it Rubio, after herself."

Tiger nodded or meowed agreement at the end of each sentence, backing her up but not interrupting.

"Then the monster looked at us. I didn't know how dangerous its eyes are. After that there was nothing until you came into the clearing and broke the spell."

"Oh, thank you! Thank you!" Tiger made as if to rush forward and embrace Pumpkin.

Phukat rose to his feet and gave the two cats a look that said 'move and you're dead.'

Pumpkin looked thoughtful. "That is some story. I don't think I believe it. But let's wait for Snowball to return." He eyed his captives suspiciously. "You two might want to come up with the truth before then." Pumpkin sat down, curling his long tail around his front paws.

Celeste's thoughts raced furiously but she couldn't come up with any explanation that wouldn't result in them losing a lot of fur and maybe an ear or an eye. Telling the truth seemed the worst possible course of action.

She watched Phukat for an opening. He had the typical slightly crossed blue eyes of poorly bred Siamese cats. This made it difficult to tell exactly where he was looking. He purred a slow, deep purr that said nothing would make him happier than to tear Celeste and Tiger apart. All trace of their former alliance against the dogs had vanished. Phukat was Pumpkin's cat one hundred percent.

After several minutes, Snowball returned, alone, to give his report to Pumpkin.

"I don't know, Boss. I followed 'em all the way through the brush to the other side. They went down to the water and most of the prints went in, including the big ones."

"What about Ruby?" Tiger asked.

Snowball shook his head. "I saw something sitting on the bank, kind of cat-shaped but it wasn't a cat like I ever saw. It had green gunk oozing off it. And underneath it crouched some kind of monster with a giant head."

"That's Ruby!" Celeste cried. She hadn't realized what a bad impression the little cat would make in her current state. "And that thing underneath her was the giant hamster. That's what it did to her. You didn't look in its eyes, did you? If you did, that might happen to you too."

Snowball looked nervously between Celeste and Tiger, who nodded agreement at everything Celeste said. "I do- do- don't *think* I did," he said. Then turning to Pumpkin, "I don't want that to happen to me. If that was Ruby, I mean, she doesn't even look like a cat anymore."

"What about the giant hamster?" Pumpkin asked, completely indifferent to Snowball's fears.

"It had big, black eyes," Snowball said. "But I didn't look at them really. I mean, it has to be looking back at you, right, for the spell to work?" he asked Celeste, his eyes full of fear.

Celeste didn't have a chance to answer. Pumpkin cuffed Snowball on the side of the head. "You're talking to me, not to her. And don't be an idiot; that's just a stupid story they made up to save their hides. Tell me about the hamster."

"This, this *thing*, didn't look like a hamster to me. My ow-ow- owner's girlfriend's kid used to have one until I ate it. Didn't make more than a mouthful. But this thing must weigh a third what I weigh, maybe three pounds. And it's all head and black feet. I didn't think it was alive until it started squeaking. Then the cat-animal—Ruby?—leaned down and licked it. Licked it!" He paused. "A cat shouldn't ever lick a hamster, Boss. Not even before he eats it."

"The monster made her do it," Celeste cut in. "She's hypnotized. Tiger and I were lucky it didn't do that to us. If you hadn't saved us, it would have come back and made us its slaves!"

"What if it comes back now?" Snowball asked.

"We should go," Celeste stood up.

Tiger followed her lead. He got to his feet and started wailing, "We should go! We should go! I don't want to be a zombie!" He took a step forward, making for the escape route behind Pumpkin and Phukat.

"Wait a minute," Pumpkin's voice bellowed with authority.

Celeste, who had been about to follow Tiger, froze. While Pumpkin and Tiger were both big orange tabbies, Celeste had never seen her friend look or sound like Pumpkin did now. She would have obeyed Pumpkin even if she'd never seen him before and he didn't have two thugs to back him up.

"No one is going anywhere until I say so," Pumpkin eyed Celeste. "I'll tell you now, little cat, I don't believe in mind control. And I sure don't believe that a rodent's mind could control a cat's. Do you hear how stupid that sounds?" He directed his last comment to Snowball. "You're telling me that you're afraid a *hamster* is going to control you with its *mind*." He laughed. "Only considering how gullible you are, it's almost believable."

The cats all sat in silence for a moment, waiting for permission to move. He looked them over, one by one. The only one who did not wither under that gaze was Phukat who, because of the problem with his eyes, might not have noticed the searing nature of his leader's look.

Pumpkin stood. "I'm going to see this thing for myself. You're all coming with me. Phukat, make sure our guests stay in line."

Leading the way, Snowball crouched and slithered down the path Ruby and the capybaras had taken. Pumpkin followed, then Celeste, then Tiger, with Phukat bringing up the rear. They emerged on a trail unfamiliar to Celeste. Using her detective skills, she determined it led to the pond since they were going downhill. She could hear traffic so they must not be far from the road.

Their progress was slow until Pumpkin grabbed Snowball by the scruff of the neck and shook him hard. "Get moving or I'll give you some incentive," Pumpkin growled.

They trotted down a muddy stretch of trail until they came
to the edge of the pool. A short distance away, along the shore,
Celeste saw the pitiful form of Ruby with little Rubio snuggled
beside her. The image made Celeste catch her breath. She hadn't
realized what a price Ruby had paid for their attempts to catch
the capybara. She didn't look like a cat anymore. To add to all of
her other injuries, she must have poked her eye on the brambles
as she and the capybaras escaped, for one eye was completely
swollen shut. A snaggletooth protruded where a cut distorted the
smooth outline of her mouth. The blunt end of her unnaturally
short tail curled up off the ground.

"Ruby!" Celeste called, forgetting her companions for a
moment.

Ruby had to turn her head a long way to bring her good eye
into position to view Celeste. She started to smile but stopped
when she noticed the other cats. "What's going on, Celeste? Why
did you bring Pumpkin?"

"I didn't mean—"

"I brought myself," Pumpkin said. "What's that thing you
have with you?"

"Nothing," Ruby pushed Rubio behind her.

"It looks like a giant hamster."

"Well, it's not. It's a puppy."

Tiger laughed. "Maybe you are hypnotized! Or can't you
see out of either eye?" He leaped forward, cutting the distance
between himself and Ruby in half. "Let me have it. What's a cat
got to do with a puppy anyway?"

"No!" Ruby stepped back, keeping herself between Pumpkin and Rubio. "You don't need a puppy either. You can't have Rubio."

"Well, well, well. Got yourself a namesake, have you?"

Celeste cringed. She might not like the capybaras but she couldn't let Pumpkin have them. If only she could figure out some way to stop him. He had Ruby trapped, dense brush on one side and the pond on the other.

Phukat moved up to stand next to Pumpkin's shoulder, backing the big cat's brute strength with his wiry agility. His sharply pointed, dark-tipped ears flicked in anticipation. "Want me to take her out, Boss?" Phukat's silky voice begged for the opportunity.

"No, I think I'll do this myself. I want to hear the little bugger squeal in my teeth."

Celeste could smell Ruby's panic. Even healthy and uninjured, she could not beat Pumpkin in a fight. In her current condition she wouldn't make it past the first swipe of her adversary's large paw.

"Wait!" Celeste cried. "That thing will mesmerize you. You haven't seen its eyes. It's dangerous!"

"I'll take my chances," Pumpkin didn't bother to turn to face Celeste. "Today is not a good day to die, Ruby. Give up the hamster."

"I can't," Ruby pleaded. "He loves me. And he's just a baby."

"That's a baby?" Pumpkin laughed. He turned to Phukat and Snowball, "Do you hear that? This one's a baby!"

The two thugs knew their job and they laughed heartily in agreement. But Celeste could see Snowball's nervousness. After a moment, he ventured, "I did see some big footprints when I tracked them, Pumpkin."

At this, the tabby swung his head around and glared at Snowball.

"Yeah, it's crazy," Snowball corrected himself quickly. "That thing's as big as a dozen hamsters already."

Pumpkin reached pouncing distance and still Celeste had not thought of a way to save either Ruby or the capy-kitten. She considered throwing herself at Pumpkin, but Phukat would tackle her before she could get near him. There was no solution that wouldn't involve at least Rubio's death and probably Ruby's. Celeste could see that Ruby would not abandon the baby capybara.

The hair all along Ruby's back rose like a Mohawk. She bared her teeth and hissed. Pumpkin didn't laugh this time, instead he pounced, aiming for Ruby's throat. He landed on her with a heavy thud that knocked her to the dirt. Rubio scuttled out from behind her, bleating in terror.

Pumpkin stood up. Blood dripped from his canine teeth. "Now for my little snack." He advanced on the capy-kitten.

Celeste moved to stop him but Phukat sprang on her, knocking her down. Tiger was similarly blocked by Snowball. With her head pressed down under Phukat's paw, Celeste couldn't see either Pumpkin or Ruby but she could hear both squeals and meows. Ruby must be fighting. Celeste's admiration for the little cat soared. Small as she was, Ruby would be a good cat to have guarding her back in a fight. If only she stood a chance against Pumpkin.

Celeste cried in sympathy each time Ruby cried. Tiger did the same. Their voices wailed out through the air like sirens on human police cars. Phukat smacked Celeste hard with his paw, claws deployed, to get her to stop, but she meowed even more loudly in pain.

It became hard to hear anything over the din of screaming cats but Celeste's sensitive ears detected a splash just as Ruby's voice silenced. She and Tiger cried even more loudly, lamenting the death of their friend. "I'll get you! I'll get you!" Tiger wailed. "You can't get away with this. Why would anyone hurt a good cat like Ruby? You are evil monsters."

Over Tiger's calls, Pumpkin yelled. "She grabbed the hamster and jumped in the water!"

Celeste freed herself from Phukat and looked out over the water. She could see Ruby swimming with Rubio in front of her.

"Don't just stand there," Pumpkin yelled. "Go after her."

Phukat took two steps away from the shore.

Snowball released Tiger and stared in disbelief at Pumpkin. "You want us to *jump in the water*?" He shook his head. "I'm a cat. I can't swim."

"All cats can swim," Pumpkin said. "Get in there after her."

Phukat took another two steps back. Snowball was closer to the water already and the Siamese was undoubtedly thinking that the farther he stood from it, the more likely Snowball would be the one who had to swim.

Celeste realized that their captors had their own problems and no longer guarded them so closely. She tried to signal to Tiger but his attention was fixed on Ruby. She couldn't make her break without him. That left only one thing to do. If she thought about it, she knew she wouldn't have the strength to do it, so she set her body in motion and allowed herself to be carried along.

Springing forward, Celeste knocked Snowball over with a thud to his shoulder. "Come on," she called to Tiger without slowing. Two more bounds and she felt the soft mud of the shore under her paws. She leaped forward as far as she could, willing herself to jump all the way to the opposite shore. She didn't make it and landed with a splash that sent her plunging under the surface.

It was her second swim in twenty-four hours. Maybe it got easier each time because it didn't seem as bad anymore. She never would have dared to take the plunge if she hadn't gotten the earlier practice. After gulping enough air to fill her lungs, she turned her head to look toward the shore.

Tiger's head bobbed in the water behind her, his big yellow eyes wide with fear, his feet kicking wildly. On the bank, Pumpkin stood with his two lackeys, pacing and yelling. Neither Snowball nor Phukat appeared willing to jump in to catch the escaped prisoners.

Turning her attention to her own progress, Celeste realized she had nearly overtaken Ruby. The younger cat's head bobbed in the water. Celeste swam to her. "Are you okay? Can you make it?"

Ruby gasped as water filled her mouth. She spit it out. "I don't know. Rubio's too little to swim. If you would help him..."

"Don't worry," Celeste assured her. "I'll take care of Rubio."

"Promise me...." Ruby struggled to get another breath. "Save Rubio. Don't let him drown."

"I promise."

Ruby pushed Rubio toward Celeste. "Keep him safe."

Celeste put her nose into the water to give the little capybara some buoyancy. When she came back up, Ruby's head was sinking under the surface. Celeste cried out but Tiger was not a good enough swimmer to help. When she released Rubio, the little kitten sank so quickly he might have been made of lead. She couldn't go after Ruby and keep Rubio afloat. A moan of defeat echoed through her body. She had to keep her promise, she had to save Rubio.

Celeste could do nothing but keep swimming, pushing Rubio ahead. The bite from Pumpkin and the subsequent struggle must have been too much for Ruby. Remorse flooded Celeste's heart. The little calico had been a nuisance, someone Celeste routinely avoided. Now she couldn't imagine not seeing her tomorrow.

They approached a dense growth of cattails marking a small island in the pond. She needed to rest. She pushed Rubio in that direction and hoped Tiger would follow. He'd had a hard couple of days too and must be as exhausted as she was.

She dragged herself on shore, pushing Rubio before her. It annoyed her that the capybara did not have a decent neck scruff to pick him up by. He whined and squealed when she sank her teeth into the skin on the back of his neck. Although she knew it hurt him, she had little choice if she wanted to move him.

Tiger crawled up beside her. "What happened to Ruby?" His words came in gasps as he struggled to get his breath.

"Eep, eep, eep," Rubio called, looking over the water. "Eeep. Eeeeep."

"She's not coming." Celeste forced herself to say. "She went under and she didn't come back up."

Tiger sank into the mud. "No. Not little Ruby."

* * *

Chapter Eight
How (not) to win a cat fight

Celeste woke to the realization that she had blacked out. The last thing she remembered was Rubio licking her face. The sensation had been oddly comforting. It didn't feel at all like a kitten's rough tongue. Instead she felt like the capy-kitten shared her loss, licking her pain away with its feeble ability to understand what had happened.

She lay in the mud on the island in the middle of the pond with Tiger at her side. It all came back to her. Ruby had drowned, leaving little Rubio in her care.

Rising to her feet, Celeste scanned the small island. She did not see Rubio. Tall weeds grew at one end where the island fell in a gentle slope to the water. Celeste began poking through them. She called for Rubio and listened for his tell-tale squeaks. Nothing.

After a few minutes, she accepted that Rubio had left the island. When Tiger came up beside her, Celeste sat down and cried. Tiger licked her shoulders to comfort her.

Tiger caught a grasshopper and gave it to her. Normally Celeste only played with the hoppy insects. Eventually they ended up dead with a leg, or a wing or even an abdomen in her stomach, more by accident than design. But she gobbled down the one Tiger gave her, which only made her more aware of her hunger. They spent the next few minutes hunting and eating grasshoppers as quickly as they were caught. As they hunted, Celeste found the place where Rubio's footprints re-entered the water. She looked across the narrow channel to the mainland; she and Tiger would have to make that swim.

When they had eaten enough to curb their hunger, the two cats sat on the shore. Celeste kept remembering how Ruby had asked her to take care of Rubio. And now she had lost them both. She thought she could see the place in the water where Ruby had gone under.

"We'd better get going," Celeste said.

They walked side-by-side down to the narrowest point. Celeste steeled herself, and when they reached the beach, she kept walking until the water became too deep and she had to swim. Tiger remained faithfully by her side.

They crawled up the bank on the mainland and shook themselves dry. Then they both stood still, lacking the will to move any further. Celeste listened to the slow plop, plop of water falling from their belly-fur into the mud. She raised her head and swiveled her ears forward. "Tiger, do you hear that?"

"You mean that clicking?"

"It's a capybara. Maybe it's Rubio." She rose and trotted off, following the sound. She heard a squeak and then the unique "eep" the capybara kittens made. Maybe she could still save Rubio.

Now she could smell them. She'd noticed before that their scent didn't carry far; a capybara must be close. She pushed through the brush with her nose and Tiger followed.

The reeds and grasses gave way to reveal a small clearing. The cats stopped in their tracks. After all they had been through, Celeste didn't think she could still be surprised, but her eyes opened wide and she momentarily forgot to breathe. On the far side of the clearing, Caplynn Rous lay nursing her many offspring. Closer to them, sprawled on the ground in an un-catlike manner, lay the bedraggled form of Ruby.

"Do you think she's dead?" Tiger asked.

"No. She's pretty badly hurt but she's still breathing. Come on."

As they walked into the clearing, one of the kittens broke away from the others and hopped up to Celeste in its weird, stumbling gait. Celeste recognized this one by the tuft of light hair between its ears. "Hello Celester." She nuzzled the little capybara.

The animal barked at her and swung its head in a low arc.

"I can't play right now. I need to check on Ruby."

When she heard her name, Ruby opened her eyes—or rather she opened the one eye that wasn't swollen shut.

"Ruby," Celeste said as she licked her cheek. "How do you feel?"

"Caplynn saved me." Ruby struggled to speak, each word coming after a gasping breath. "Where's Rubio?"

Knowing Ruby lived did nothing to alleviate Celeste's guilt. Her friend had suffered serious injury to protect the capybara kitten and she had lost it.

"We're looking for him," Tiger said.

"I'm sure he's okay," Celeste added. "We got him to an island in the pond but then he disappeared."

Ruby didn't reply. Her eye had closed and only her labored breathing and a small gasp indicated she understood what they said.

"Ruby needs a vet," Tiger said.

This time the tom's statement of the obvious wrenched Celeste's heart. If only Ruby could come out of this with just the tip of her tail missing! "We have to find some humans and bring them here. There are probably some walking or jogging around the apartment complex. Do you think you can find a human while I search for Rubio?"

"Don't worry, Celeste. You and Ruby can count on me." Tiger raised his tail and trotted off.

Returning to Ruby, Celeste licked some of the blood off her neck. The puncture marks were small but deep. Since Ruby had been in the water, Celeste couldn't tell how much blood she had lost, but at least she was not bleeding now. "Don't worry, Ruby. I'll find Rubio."

As she turned to leave, Celeste almost stepped on Celester. The little capybara looked up at her with its dark pit eyes and squeaked. It raised a front paw and waved it playfully.

Celeste nuzzled her namesake and licked him on his blunt snout. "I'll be back, little guy. Keep an eye on Ruby for me."

* * *

The sun shone over the horizon when Celeste finally heard the characteristic eeping of a baby capybara. Not wanting to frighten it, she crept toward the sound. The little one had roamed a great distance for such a small animal. They were almost back to Celeste's apartment; she could see yellow light from the covered parking. A car engine started.

Celeste's head shot up. Her heart pounded against her ribs at twice its normal rate. The tiny capy-kitten was in the parking lot. Rushing forward, Celeste plunged through the bars of the fence and onto the pavement. She spun around, looking for Rubio.

"Nice to see you again, Celeste. How did that dip in the pond go?"

Celeste jerked to a stop. Before her stood Phukat, all smirks and self-confidence, his crossed eyes looking vaguely in her direction. Under one brutal paw squirmed the bloodied form of Rubio, eeping as if his life depended on it.

"Come to get your little pet?" Phukat dug his claws into his captive to make him screech louder.

"Let him go." Celeste's voice surprised her; it carried no hint of the terror she felt.

"I don't think so. Pumpkin wants this little morsel." The cat shrugged. "And there might be leftovers. I'm curious about the flavor of giant hamster myself."

Without thinking, Celeste charged. She leaped into the air and came down on Phukat's back, claws extended and a war cry issuing from her throat. Surprise was on her side and she managed to knock Phukat off his feet, freeing Rubio.

Phukat sprang up, claws flying. His right paw raked down on Celeste's leg, right over the dog bite. Her hind quarters gave under her, overcome by the double wound and the weight of the larger cat. She tried to twist away but Phukat clung to her, pulling himself forward to get a bite on her neck. She kicked out and connected with the inner thigh of his right leg. Phukat wailed. He slid off her back and began circling toward her head.

"I don't want a fight," Celeste said.

"That's funny, 'cause you picked this one." Phukat spat the words at her.

"Just give me the capy-kitten."

"What have you got to trade?"

"I let you walk away."

"Ha! That's a good one. Pumpkin wants that animal and I'd rather fight you than him. You're half his weight and not one-tenth his determination. I think things are looking good for me right now." He charged, rearing in the air with his front paws raised and his claws glistening.

Celeste lunged. Her teeth sank into Phukat's right foreleg. Phukat countered, kicking her in the stomach with both hind feet, but Celeste did not let go. She shook her head, digging her teeth in more deeply. Her left canine tooth hit something hard.

Phukat buried his teeth in Celeste's head, taking her whole ear into his mouth. Pain blinded her but she didn't release her hold. She twisted under him, pulling his leg with her and knocking the Siamese off balance.

Her teeth shifted as Phukat tried to pull away. The sharp points of her incisors found a ridge in the bone. Celeste scrunched her eyes, her whiskers lay flat against her cheeks.

Crack! The sound came through her jaw first, then echoed in her ears. Under her teeth, she felt the sharp crack of breaking bone. She snapped her jaw open. Phukat's scream echoed across the parking lot. Celeste rolled to her feet to find her enemy hissing and spitting as he backed away, his right front paw dangling helplessly.

Celeste staggered to Rubio. Blood soaked the coarse fur behind his head and he had a streak of red down his side. She picked him up by the neck, no doubt inflicting more harm on the hapless kitten, but she had no choice. She needed to get the two of them home. Mother and Father and human Celeste would take care of them.

She could see her building. A thin line of discolored paint from the recent flood pointed out her apartment. If only she could make it there. With each step Celeste got weaker. Her pain and the shrill calls of the baby capybara blurred her consciousness. She reached the base of the stairs and lifted Rubio onto the first step.

"Arf! Arf, arf, arf!"

Celeste whipped around, causing her vision to spin. When her eyes finally focused she saw the two wiener dogs rushing across the parking lot.

"Arf, arf, arf, arf!"

Celeste pushed Rubio onto the second step. She climbed up and stood with Rubio under her belly. Stupid little dogs. After all she'd been through, they were not going to get her or the capy-kitten.

The dogs reached the stairs and began hopping like vicious wind-up toys, snapping at Celeste with their long snouts with lulling red tongues and barking the whole time.

Celeste pinned her ears and arched her back. Each time a dog snapped at her, it got a pawfull of claws. They didn't manage to land a single bite on either her or Rubio.

But the dachshunds had infinite energy and Celeste was already tired. The dogs were playing with her. They knew she couldn't keep it up.

"What's going on here?" Out of the corner of her eye, Celeste saw Kristina Colorado standing in her apartment doorway. "Oh no! Celeste, is that you?" She rushed forward, kicking the dogs away. "Git! Git! Why can't people control their animals?" The dogs disappeared among the parked cars.

Kristina knelt next to Celeste. "Poor little kitty. Look at you! What a mess. And what's this?" Her face scrunched up. She looked at Celeste then back to Rubio. "What is this thing,

Celeste? You were protecting it? Okay. Let's get the two of you upstairs. Philip and Monica will know what to do."

* * *

Celeste's head pounded, protesting the noisy cries that sent shock waves from her eardrums to her brain. She moaned and tried to roll over but found herself too weak to move. "I must be dead."

"You're not dead," a disembodied voice floated across the void.

The plaintive meows of many cats threatened to drown her mind. "Am I at the pound?"

"You're not at the pound." The voice sounded like Ruby.

"Then where am I?"

"The emergency vet clinic."

Celeste shuddered. "How did I get here?"

"When they brought you in, your human said you were in a dog fight but the vet said your wounds look more like they're from a cat."

It came back to Celeste in a flash. "What happened to Rubio?" she cried. "Is he okay?" Her head spinning, Celeste rose to a sitting position. "Ruby, is that you?"

"Yes."

"You're all right? What happened?"

"Well, I guess I'm down to seven lives. Maybe six. But I'm feeling better now. And the emergency vet isn't so bad after all."

"But what happened?"

"You went to look for Rubio—and I guess you found him, right?—and Tiger went to get help. After a while he came back with Mr. Levan, that's the man who owns Caplynn Rous and the capy-kittens. He was nice. He herded Caplynn into the back of his van and the kittens followed. Once he'd rounded them all up he came back for me. He wrapped me in his own jacket and put me on the front seat. He kept petting me and telling me to hold on the whole way to the vet. When we got here, he said, 'Do whatever it takes, just get this cat well.'"

Ruby went on and on, telling all the details of her medical treatment, how nice Mr. Levan was, how he brought Celester in to keep her company during the early stages of her recovery, how many stitches she had and when they would come out. "Then you came in," Ruby concluded.

"And?" Celeste said when it became clear Ruby would not continue without prompting.

"Oh. Human Celeste came in with you and her father and the vet. From what they said, I gathered your neighbor rescued you and Rubio from some dogs. But when the vet said you'd been in a fight with another cat, I figured it must have been Phukat or Pumpkin—I don't think Snowball has the guts for a real fight. You had surgery and stitches on your stomach and your head. That's all I know."

"Did they say how Rubio is? Phukat got him. He's not hurt too badly is he?"

"I don't think so. Human Celeste and Mr. Levan didn't seem too worried about him. I think he had to see the vet though. He got some shots or something. Thank you for taking care of him."

Celeste didn't reply. She hadn't taken good care of Rubio. Even if Ruby didn't blame her, it was her fault that Phukat got hold of the capybara at all.

The cries continued to echo from the other cages. Some were simply moans of pain, others were calls for loved ones to come rescue them, and some were mournful laments. Celeste could not stay positive in such a place. Hearing Ruby hum the joyful tune of *Every Cat Has His Day* from her cage did not brighten Celeste's spirits; it just made her lonelier. She missed human Celeste. And Father and Mother. She even missed Celestina a little. She would much rather hear her stupid hamster wheel than the constant cries of her fellow patients.

"Celeste?" Ruby said in the middle of the night when nearly all the other cats were asleep. "Are you awake?"

Celeste grunted a reply.

"I just wanted to say thanks for letting me go on the capybara hunt with you."

"What?"

"I know I'm not a very good hunter. I'm not quiet enough or big and strong like Tiger and I don't have the patience. But you took me anyway. And I learned a lot. You're a smart cat, Celeste. I wish I could be more like you."

Having no response to this, Celeste sank back down and tried to sleep.

* * *

Morning brought fresh food and water. Celeste devoured everything set before her. She hadn't eaten anything except grasshoppers in the last two days.

Later the vet came and checked each of the cats. Celeste had an oblique view as he brought out Ruby and placed her on the exam table. Ruby's tail was bandaged again; she had a cone on her head; white bandaging encircled her middle; and one eye had a big white patch on it. If that weren't enough, much of her hair had been shaved.

The vet, a young man with black hair and a bushy mustache, scratched her cheek while Ruby purred wildly. "You're a special cat, aren't you? Somebody really beat you up but you're too tough to die. I'd call you Leprechaun if you were my cat."

Ruby purred and rubbed her head against his hand and arm. "See how nice he is?" she called to Celeste. "He loves me."

When her turn came, Celeste cowered at the back of her cage. She did not trust the vet, no matter what Ruby said. She clawed at his arms and tried to jump down. "Let me go! Let me go!" she called, over and over again. Even if humans could understand cats, he probably wouldn't care that she didn't want to be picked up. But in her weakened state she could do little to protect herself and the vet wore thick gloves. She sank her teeth into them but they weren't long enough to go all the way through.

"You've got more spunk than I expected." The vet turned her over and examined her stomach. "Quite the resilient little kitty. I guess your owners were right, nothing can keep you down for long. You have some nasty wounds but it looks like you're going to be fine, minus some damage to the ear."

Celeste hissed. Didn't he know cats don't like to be turned over? Did he want to torment her? And what did he mean about her ear? Celeste rubbed her bandaged head. Was her ear under there?

Late in the afternoon she heard human Celeste's voice. She stood up in her cage, put her paws on the wire mesh door and meowed with all her might. "I'm in here! Come save me!"

The door opened and human Celeste raced in, looking up and down through the cages. Celeste cried and cried but her calls were lost amid the wailing echoes of other patients.

Human Celeste saw Ruby before she found cat Celeste. "Look Daddy! That's Audrey's cat! Look! Look! She has a bandage on her tail. Ruby? Is that you?"

After a moment, human Celeste left Ruby and found Celeste. "There you are, you pretty cat. You are so brave! You saved that baby capybara. You fought off dogs. Oh, Celeste, you are the best cat in the whole world!" She turned to face Father. "Can we take her home now?"

"In a minute. We have to wait for the technician to get her out."

"And we can't leave without Ruby, Daddy. Audrey's been so worried about her."

"Well, I don't know. We didn't bring her in. Whoever did is probably the one who can check her out. We can't be sure it really is Ruby."

"It's me! It's me!" Ruby cried from her cage. "Celeste, don't leave without me. How will Audrey ever find me here? I want to go home."

Celeste heard human voices in the hallway. One she recognized as the woman who had given her breakfast. The other was familiar but she couldn't place it. Then she heard "eep, eeep." She jumped to her feet. "Ruby, did you hear that? It's Rubio!"

The technician entered the room with Mr. Levan in tow. Cradled in Mr. Levan's arms was Rubio, all bandaged up but eeping happily.

"I'm glad I caught you here," Mr. Levan said to Father. "I wanted to thank you again. Your cat saved this little guy's life. I must say, cats have been acting strangely lately. Can't hardly tell what they might do next. But yours and this one," he pointed to Ruby's cage, "and the big tabby that ran off, well, they done some pretty good things for me and my rodents."

"You brought Ruby in?" human Celeste asked.

"That her name? Yeah, found her with my capys, one of them tucked right up against her like she was its momma. And look at her. I reckon she fought off a whole army of cats or maybe a couple dogs. Guess I can use her as a guard cat if I can't find her owners."

"Audrey owns me!" Ruby cried from her cage. "I want to go back to Audrey."

"I know her owner. She's in my class."

"Well, that's lucky then, isn't it? Doc says I can check her out. If you'll help me, I'll get her back home where she belongs."

It seemed like forever before they completed her final checkup and all the paperwork was filled out so she could go home. She was still weak, so she didn't protest when human Celeste wrapped her in a towel and put her in a roomy cat carrier.

Mr. Levan followed behind in his white van as they drove to the apartment complex.

They went to Ruby's house first. Audrey and Sheldon ran from their rooms when they heard Ruby was back. They brought her in and treated her like a queen.

Mr. Levan set Rubio down. He went straight to Ruby and snuggled against her, clicking joyfully. "Well, don't that beat all? That little capy likes your cat better than his own momma, and that's a fact."

The humans sat around talking for a long while. They let Celeste and Ruby lie together on the floor and Rubio plopped down between them.

Celeste drifted in and out of wakefulness. At one point Ruby pushed her in the shoulder with her front paw. "Look. Tiger's at the glass door."

It took all her strength, but Celeste lifted her head and smiled at her friend. She felt a warm wash of happiness that soon ushered her back to sleep.

The next time she awoke, Celeste found herself lying in her favorite sunny spot on the window seat in her room. A small bowl of water and another of tuna were nearby. The hamster wheel squeaked. Celeste purred and went back to sleep.

* * *

Epilogue

The setting sun shone warmly through the glass and onto Celeste's dark fur. She shook the last remnants of sleep from her eyes and rose to her feet. A long stretch of her thin form, her claws scraping the paint on the window seat, and she was ready to start a new adventure.

She hopped down to the carpeted floor and walked to the cage where Celestina slept the day away. She still didn't see the point of a pet hamster but she no longer detested Celestina. In some small way the dwarf hamster reminded her of its giant cousins and that made her smile.

She pushed her way through the cat door. The mournful twang of country music from a distant apartment enveloped her.

When she reached the bottom of the stairs she sat down on the sidewalk and joined the cat accompaniment, raising her voice into the twilight. Pumpkin and Snowball were sitting in their usual positions on the fence. Phukat no longer attended. His owners had turned him into an indoor cat.

Pumpkin and his gang didn't frighten Celeste anymore. She'd seen they were no stronger, braver or smarter than she was.

Tiger appeared and joined in beside her.

A few minutes later, Ruby bounced up, her mouth full of dead leaves she had caught on the way over.

"What are we going to do tonight?" Tiger asked.

Ruby spit out the leaves, *"Every day's a new adventure for the cats who caught a hamster."*

Celeste flicked her ears, although the right one hardly moved since her fight with Phukat. "That's not bad, but if you're going to make up new cat sayings, they should apply to more than just the three of us."

"I know," Ruby said, "but practice makes perfect."

Celeste nodded. Ruby had developed an expertise in human sayings as well.

"So what *are* we going to do tonight?" Ruby asked.

"I was thinking of going to the other side of the highway."

Ruby gasped. "You mean cross the road? We'll be killed."

Tiger laughed. "I remember. We can use the tunnel, right Celeste? No one's been to the other side since they built the road."

"*Where no cat's gone, we bravely go!*" Ruby said.

Celeste purred and repeated the new saying.

"We can make that our motto," Tiger said. "We're the cats who bravely go where no cats have gone before."

"I like it," Celeste said. She didn't mean just the new motto.

* * *

Author Bio

Melanie Typaldos has loved all types of animals for as long
as she can remember. She currently lives in Buda, Texas with her
husband Rick, her capybara, Caplin Rous, two rainbow boas,
two leopard tortoises and four horses.

About Caplin Rous and Pet Capybaras

To learn more about Caplin Rous, who served as the model for
the capybaras in this book, please go to www.GiantHamster.com
or view videos of his life at www.YouTube.com/CaplinCapybara.

I highly recommend the book Capyboppy by Bill Peet that
served as our guide as we raised Caplin Rous.

* * *

10436573R00084

Made in the USA
Charleston, SC
04 December 2011